Y0-BZB-846

The

ESSENTIAL COLLECTION

Shipment One

A Little Bit Country
Country Bride
Wanted: Perfect Partner
Cindy and the Prince
Some Kind of Wonderful
The Courtship of Carol Sommars

Shipment Two

Navy Wife
Navy Blues
Navy Brat
Navy Woman
Navy Baby
Navy Husband

Shipment Three

Yours and Mine
The Bachelor Prince
Denim and Diamonds
The Wyoming Kid
The Man You'll Marry
Marriage Wanted
Laughter in the Rain

Shipment Four

The Cowboy's Lady
The Sheriff Takes a Wife
Marriage of Inconvenience
Stand-In Wife
Bride on the Loose
Same Time, Next Year

Shipment Five

Rainy Day Kisses
Mail-Order Bride
The Matchmakers
Father's Day
A Friend or Two
No Competition

Shipment Six

First Comes Marriage
White Lace and Promises
Friends—and Then Some
The Way to a Man's Heart
Hasty Wedding
That Wintry Feeling
Those Christmas Angels

Shipment Seven

Borrowed Dreams
Starlight
Promise Me Forever
Shadow Chasing
For All My Tomorrows
The Playboy and the Widow

Shipment Eight

Fallen Angel
Yesterday's Hero
Reflections of Yesterday
All Things Considered
The Trouble With Caasi
Almost Paradise

ESSENTIAL COLLECTION

#1 *New York Times* Bestselling Author

DEBBIE MACOMBER

The Bachelor PRINCE

H HARLEQUIN®
™ESSENTIAL DEBBIE MACOMBER COLLECTION

Recycling programs
for this product may
not exist in your area.

ISBN-13: 978-0-373-47284-0

THE BACHELOR PRINCE

Printed in U.S.A.

DEBBIE MACOMBER

is a number one *New York Times* and *USA TODAY* best-selling author. Her books include *1225 Christmas Tree Lane, 1105 Yakima Street, A Turn in the Road, Hannah's List* and *Debbie Macomber's Christmas Cookbook,* as well as *Twenty Wishes, Summer on Blossom Street* and *Call Me Mrs. Miracle.* She has become a leading voice in women's fiction worldwide and her work has appeared on every major bestseller list, including those of the *New York Times, USA TODAY, Publishers Weekly* and *Entertainment Weekly.* She is a multiple award winner, and won the 2005 Quill Award for Best Romance. There are more than one hundred million copies of her books in print. Two of her Harlequin MIRA Christmas titles have been made into Hallmark Channel Original Movies, and the Hallmark Channel has launched a series based on her bestselling Cedar Cove series. For more information on Debbie and her books, visit her website, www.debbiemacomber.com.

Prologue

Prince Stefano Giorgio Paolo needed a wife. A very rich one. And soon.

He couldn't put off the inevitability of marriage any longer, not if he planned to save his country from the international embarrassment of bankruptcy.

Tightly clenching the Minister of Finance's latest report, he paced the royal office, his mind racing as he trod past the series of six-foot sandstone windows adorned with heavy red draperies.

The view of the courtyard with the huge stone fountain, which dated from the seventeenth century, escaped his attention. At one time the scene below would have given him great joy. But no longer. Now it brought a heaviness to his chest. All because the courtyard was empty of tourists.

San Lorenzo, a tiny European principality, had once thrived as a fairytale kingdom, and drawn hordes of sightseers from all across the globe. But with the civil unrest in the Balkan states so close to its borders, the tourists stayed away.

It didn't help that San Lorenzo had no international airport of its own and the closest one was now closed to commercial traffic because of the fighting.

A knock against the heavy oak door distracted him. "Yes," Stefano blurted out impatiently. He'd left word he wasn't to be disturbed. Only a fool would dare interrupt him.

His personal secretary and traveling companion, Pietro, stepped inside the room. Stefano amended his earlier thought. Only a fool *or a friend* would dare intrude on him now.

"I thought you might need this," Pietro said, carrying in an elaborate silver tray with two glasses and a cut-crystal decanter.

"You know I don't drink during the day," Stefano chastised, but without any real censure.

"Generally that's true," Pietro agreed, "but I also know you're thinking about marriage, and the subject, as always, depresses you."

"Once again you're right, my friend." His shoulders sagging, Stefano rubbed a hand over his face and stared out the window at his small kingdom.

"Have you made your decision?" Pietro asked, lifting the stopper from the decanter and splashing two fingers into the glasses. He handed the first to Stefano, who gratefully accepted it.

"Do I have any choice, but to marry?" He felt as if he were sentencing himself to the gallows. He savored his life as a bachelor, and the freedom it offered him to sample the favors of some of the world's most beautiful women.

Frankly, he enjoyed the title of the Bachelor Prince that the tabloids had bestowed on him. The papers, if they were to be believed, claimed he was the perfect romantic prince. They touted him as tall, dark and handsome, with enough charm to sink a flotilla.

It was true he was tall—six foot two—and his skin was tanned a healthy shade of bronze from the many hours he spent out-of-doors. The handsome part, he took with a grain of salt. His features were aristocratic, he supposed. His forehead was high and his chin stately, but then his family had reined over San Lorenzo for nearly seven hundred years.

"Have you decided upon the lucky lady?" Pietro asked in that casual way of his that made Stefano's most troublesome worries appear minimal.

Frowning, Stefano thought for a moment, one hand clenched behind his back. "No." He gestured with his drink toward his friend. "I prefer to marry an American," he decided suddenly.

"Having attended Duke University, you're well acquainted with their ways. American women can be most charming."

Stefano slapped his drink down on the desk. "I don't need charm, I need money."

"Trust me, Stefano, I know that." Pietro reached inside his perfectly tailored black suit and withdrew a piece of paper. "I've taken the liberty of listing several eligible American women for your consideration."

Stefano paused and steadily regarded his friend. Oftentimes he wondered if Pietro could read his mind. "How well you know me."

Pietro bowed slightly. "It was a lucky guess."

Stefano laughed, doubting that. Pietro was much too thorough to leave anything to guesswork. In some ways his secretary knew him better than he did himself.

Like a spoiled child, Stefano had put off dealing with the unpleasantness of his situation. He sat down and rested against the back of the plush velvet chair. "Tell me what you've learned."

"There are a number of excellent young women from whom to choose," Pietro began.

For the next half hour, his secretary provided him with a list of names and the information he'd collected on each woman. There wasn't one who even mildly captured Stefano's curiosity. Perhaps Stefano was just old-fashioned enough to believe in marrying for love. When it came to choosing a wife, he would have preferred to cherish his bride with all his heart and soul, without an eye on her purse strings. But courtly ideals weren't going to save San Lorenzo.

"Well?" Pietro asked, when he'd finished.

Stefano gestured weakly with his hand. "You choose."

Pietro's eyebrows arched. "As you wish."

His companion ran his index finger down the list, pausing at one name and then another. His frown grew darker. Gauging from his reaction, Pietro was having as difficult time choosing as Stefano.

"Priscilla Rutherford," Pietro announced thoughtfully.

"Priscilla," Stefano repeated, attempting to remember what he could about the woman. "The shipping magnate's daughter?"

"She's the one." Having made his decision, Pietro relaxed and sampled the first taste of his drink.

"Why her?"

Pietro shrugged. "I'm not sure. I've seen her picture."

"She's beautiful?"

It took Pietro a moment to respond. "Yes."

"You don't sound convinced."

One side of Pietro's mouth quirked upward. "She's not a flawless beauty, if that's what you want, but she's a gentle, kind woman all San Lorenzo will love."

"Do you have as much faith she'll fall in love with me?" Stefano asked.

"But, of course." Pietro crossed to the other side of the room and pulled open a drawer. "I've even come up with a way for the two of you to meet."

Stefano slowly shook his head. "You never cease to amaze me, my friend."

"Do you remember the letter we received last week from Ms. Marshall from Seattle?"

"Marshall, Marshall," Stefano repeated, running the name through his memory. "Wasn't she the one who wrote to invite me as her guest of honor to some kind of conference? Some group, something nonsensical...I don't recall what—only that I'd rather be shot than attend."

"She's the one, and it was a Romance Lovers' Convention."

"I sincerely hope you declined," Stefano said with an elongated sigh. "For the love of heaven, I have no time for such nonsense." Romance had no place in the life of a man who was forced to marry for money.

"Fortunately, I haven't responded one way or the other."

"Fortunately?" Stefano eyed his companion wearily.

"I have it on good authority that Priscilla Rutherford will be attending the convention. It would be the ideal way of casually meeting her."

Stefano resumed his pacing, circling his desk a number of times, his hands clasped behind his back. "You can't be serious? The Marshall woman had come up with some ridiculous idea of raffling off a date with me. Dear sweet heaven, Pietro, has it come to this?"

"This conference can help you achieve your goal."

Stefano's gaze narrowed. Surely his friend wasn't serious. He had no desire to stand on the auction block and be awarded to the highest bidder.

"The Romance Lovers' get-together offers you the perfect opportunity to meet Priscilla Rutherford," Pietro reiterated.

"You're serious?"

"Yes, Your Highness, I am."

It was the reference to his title that told him exactly how sincere Pietro was. "See to the arrangements, then," Stefano murmured. This had to be the low point of his life. He was about to become a sideshow at the circus, but if that was what it took to save his country, than Stefano would gladly sacrifice his considerable pride.

One

"The phone's for you."

Hope Jordan glanced irritably toward the wall of her minute coffee shop on Seattle's Fifth Avenue and dragged her wet hands across the white butcher's apron tied about her waist. She hurried toward the phone and reached for the receiver.

"Hello, Mom," she said, not waiting for her mother to announce herself.

"How'd you know it was me?" Doris Jordan asked, her voice revealing her surprise.

"Because no one else phones me when I'm this busy."

"I'm sorry, sweetheart," her mother said, not sounding the least bit contrite, "but you work too hard as it is."

"Mom, unless this is really important, I have to get off the phone. I've got three runners waiting for orders." Hope smiled apologetically toward the trio.

"You'll phone me back?"

"Yes…I promise. But sometime this afternoon, all right?"

"Sure. It's important, Hope. I'll give you the details later, but I want you to know that I've invested twenty-five dollars in tickets to win a date with Prince Stefano Giorgio Paolo of San Lorenzo."

Hope's head bobbed with each one of his names. She'd recently read a lengthy article about Prince Stefano, and his beautiful country. "You want to date someone young enough to be your son?"

"No," Doris said with an impatient sigh. "I bought the tickets for *you*."

"Mom…"

The line went abruptly dead. Hope stared at the phone for several seconds before replacing the receiver. Her mother was bound and determined to see her married, but buying her raffle tickets for a date was "one step over the line" of what Hope found acceptable.

Not that it would do her any good to argue. Her mother wanted her married. The wedding itself wasn't the important point. Grandchildren were. Her mother's three closest friends were all grandmothers. It had become a matter of social status for Doris to see Hope married and pregnant. In that order, of course. And if Hope needed a bit of encouragement along the way, well, Doris was more than happy to supply it. Unfortunately, her means of nudging Hope toward marital bliss bordered on meddling into her already-complicated life.

"We're ready anytime you are," Jimmy, the lovable nineteen-year-old college student, said with a mildly sarcastic smile.

"All right, all right," Hope muttered, lifting the thick paper cups holding a variety of coffees and carrying them from the counter to the waiting trays.

"The idea is to deliver them while they're hot," Jimmy reminded her.

Hope poked his ribs with the sharp end of her elbow.

"Hey," Jimmy protested, "what was that for?"

"Just a little incentive to get you to move faster," she said, grinning broadly.

"I'm outta here."

"That's the idea, Jimmy, my boy." She laughed as he rushed out the back door toward the Federal Building, where the majority of his thirsty clients waited.

When this last batch of runners was out the door, Hope brewed herself a latte and slumped into a chair. The morning rush was a killer.

Coffee Break, Incorporated, had been an idea whose time had come, if sales these past few months were any indication. Hope had started the business with a staff of three who made daily exotic coffee and latte deliveries to the office buildings around Seattle's thriving downtown area.

Soon she'd added a variety of low-fat muffins and other products to the menu and expanded to fifteen runners, who serviced a number of businesses each morning and midafternoon.

"What's wrong?" Lindy, the woman who baked the world's greatest muffins, asked as she pulled out a chair and plopped herself down next to Hope.

Hope flip-flopped her hand, too tired to complain. "My mother's up to her old tricks."

"Has she found another matchmaker?"

Hope was tempted to smile at the memory. Unfortunately, the woman at the matchmaking service hadn't completely understood that the men Doris wanted were meant for her daughter. Consequently Hope had been matched with a man sixty-three years old. Doris had been outraged and demanded her money back. But in the end, it had worked out for the best. The gentleman had taken a fancy to Doris and the two had dined together several times over the winter months.

"That was last time," Hope said.

"Did she arrange another date for you with her doctor's nephew?"

Despite her fatigue, Hope was tempted to laugh outright this time. "That mistake isn't likely to be repeated, either." Her dear, sweet, matchmaking mother had learned a lesson with that fiasco. Doris had insisted Hope meet Arnold Something-or-other. A doctor's nephew was sure to be a real catch, the perfect husband for her stubborn daughter.

Fool that she was, Hope had agreed to the blind date because her mother had been so excited. Doris had made it sound as if she'd miraculously stumbled upon the perfect man for Hope. If she agreed to just one date, then Hope would realize it herself.

Unfortunately, Arnold was a kleptomaniac and was wanted by the authorities for questioning in three different states. The date had been a nightmare from beginning to end. The moment they sat down in the restaurant, Arnold started lining his pockets with pink packages of artificial sweetener. Hope could see this man was no prince.

"Mom's on a different kick this time," Hope said, musing that her mother was determined to find her a prince, only this time it was for real.

Lindy handed her a fresh applesauce-

and-raisin muffin still warm from the oven. "What's she up to now?"

"I'm not entirely sure," Hope said, lifting her tired feet from the floor and securing them in the seat of the chair across from her. "It was something ridiculous about buying raffle tickets for a date with a prince."

"Hey," Lindy said, taking notice, "I read about that. It's part of the Madeline Marshall Romance Lovers' Convention that's going on at the Convention Center next week."

"The what?" Hope brushed a stray strand of blond hair from her forehead.

"Come on, Hope, you must have heard about the conference. The newspeople have been having a heyday with this all week. It starts Thursday evening with a fancy cocktail party. Romance writers from all over the world are flying in to meet their fans. Why, it's the biggest thing to hit Seattle since the World's Fair."

"You've got to be joking."

"I'm not. Romance novels are big business. Bigger than the man on the street realizes."

"Are you telling me that you read romances?" Hope asked. Lindy? Her down-to-earth baker? It didn't gel.

"Of course I do. You mean you don't?"

"Heavens, no," Hope said, shaking her head. "I don't have time to read anything right now." The demands of her business left little time for leisure activities.

"Then you're missing out, girl. Everyone needs to kick off their shoes and escape from the harsh realities of the world every now and again."

"But romance novels?" Her mother had been hooked on the books for years, reading them for therapy after Hope's father had passed away. Although Doris had brought several of her favorite novels to her daughter, Hope had never taken the time to read one. Most of her reading material consisted of magazine articles and nonfiction.

"Do you have something against romance novels?" the talented baker asked, standing. In her defense of the reading material, Lindy dug her fist into her hip and glared down at her employer.

It was all Hope could do not to laugh. Lindy's tall white baker's hat was askew, and her eyes flashed with righteous zeal. Apparently her friend took the subject seriously.

"I didn't mean to offend you," Hope offered as a means of keeping the peace.

"You didn't," Lindy was quick to assure her, "but having someone trash romance novels without ever having read them is a pet peeve of mine."

"I'll give one a try someday," Hope promised, but doubted that it would be anytime soon. Romance didn't interest her. Perhaps later, when Coffee Break,

Incorporated, was firmly on its feet, she'd consider searching for a husband.

"I bought a raffle ticket myself," Lindy announced sheepishly. "I don't know what I'd do if I won. I swear Prince Stefano is the handsomest man alive."

Hope had seen his picture often enough in the tabloids to agree with her friend's assessment. The prince was said to be the world's most eligible bachelor. "But if you won the date with him, what would you have to talk about?"

Lindy wiggled her eyebrows suggestively. "Talk? Are you nuts? If I won the date with Prince Stefano, I wouldn't waste precious time talking."

Hope laughed, then shook her head. "Of course you'd talk. That's the point of the evening, isn't it?"

A dreamy look came over Hope's friend. "Even if we did nothing but sit across the table and stare at one another all evening, I'd be thrilled."

Not Hope. If she was going to date a prince, she'd make sure the time was well spent. Oh, good grief, she was actually contemplating what it would be like. Clearly she'd been breathing too many fumes from the espresso machine.

"You won't need to call your mother back," Lindy announced all at once.

"Why not?"

"Because I just saw her crossing the street."

Hope walked over to the picture window in front of her shop. Sure enough, her dear, sweet mother was heading straight for Coffee Break, Incorporated.

"Mom," Hope breathed when the front door opened, "what are you doing here?"

"I thought I'd come see my only child who never visits her mother anymore."

The hint of guilt hung in the air like a

low-lying cloud. Hope didn't think now was the time to mention that each visit had been turned into another match-making opportunity. The last two trips home had been enough to keep Hope away for life.

"Mom, you know how busy I've been this summer. Besides, I talked to you no more than twenty minutes ago. Didn't you trust me to call you back?"

"I didn't want to chance it. Besides I was in the neighborhood."

Her mother avoided trips downtown like the plague. "What are you doing here?"

"Hazel and I came down to that fancy hotel on Fourth Street to make reservations for next week. Gladys and Betty, Hazel and I decided to spring for the big bucks and stay in the hotel for the conference."

"You're actually going to stay at a hotel in Seattle? We *live* in Seattle."

"We want to network. Who knows all

the fun we'd miss if we had to catch the five o'clock bus back to Lake City? We decided not to chance it."

"I see," Hope said, but she wasn't entirely sure she did.

"By dividing the price of the room four ways, it costs hardly anything. You can't blame us for wanting to be where the action is, now can you?"

"Where's Hazel?"

"I left her at the hotel. She's checking out the room they're giving us. Rumor has it Prince Stefano's suite is on the nineteenth floor." She paused and Hope swore her eyes sparked with mischief. "Hazel made up a story about her blood pressure and the medication she's taking. She insisted the higher the room, the better it is for her heart." A smile dimpled each of Doris's tanned cheeks. "It worked. Our room's on the eighteenth floor."

Hope could see it all now. Four retired schoolteachers lurking in corridors waiting for a glimpse of Prince Stefano. "So you're going to be rubbing shoulders with royalty."

"Just think of it, Hope. We might run in to the prince on the elevator."

"Indeed you might." Her mother sounded like a star-crazed teenager waiting for a glimpse of her favorite rock star.

"It's all for fun, Hope." She glanced at her daughter as if she feared Hope would say she was acting like an old lady.

"I think it's great, Mom," she said, resisting the urge to laugh. "You and your friends will have the time of your lives."

"You don't think we're a bunch of old biddies, do you?"

"Of course not."

"We're so excited."

"About meeting the prince?"

"That, too, but the opportunity to see all our favorite romance writers, and get their autographs. It's like a dream come true."

"You're going to have the time of your life."

Her mother didn't seem to hear her. All at once her face grew somber. "I always said someday your prince would come, didn't I, Hope? Now the time has come. He's going to fall head over heels in love with you, sweetheart."

Already Hope could see the wheels turning in her mother's fevered brain. It'd be best if she could root Doris in a bit of reality. "Mother, my winning the date with Prince Stefano is a long shot. I imagine they've sold a thousand chances."

"More," Doris said confidently. "It doesn't matter. You're going to win."

It wouldn't do any good to point out the mathematical odds of that happening were astronomical. Letting her mother dream wasn't going to hurt anything, Hope supposed. The whole thing was harmless. Hope had as much a chance of winning as the man in the moon.

"You'll be there for the drawing, won't you?"

"When?" Hope had no intention of attending, but she didn't want to tell her mother that.

"The lucky winner will be announced Thursday night at the cocktail party."

"I can't," she said automatically. "I'm meeting with my accountant to go over this quarter's taxes. You'll stand in for me, won't you?"

"If I must." Doris looked a bit disappointed, but Hope could see that the more her mother thought about it, the better she liked the idea. "Naturally, Hazel and the others would want to meet him."

"Naturally," Hope concurred. "I'll tell you what, Mom. If I win the date with Prince Stefano, I'll be sure that the four of you have a chance to chat with the prince, and it won't be in any elevator." It was easy to be generous when it cost her nothing.

Doris's face broke into a smile as wide as the Grand Canyon. "Wouldn't that be a kick."

Hope was convinced it would.

Prince Stefano looked out over the crowded ballroom floor and felt a cold chill race down his spine. Glasses clinked, champagne bubbled. Lights glowed and warmed the room from the huge crystal chandeliers. Stefano swore the eyes of a thousand women followed his every move.

He wasn't a man who frightened easily, but this situation was enough to try any man's soul. Stefano didn't doubt that if he were to stumble from the security of the stage, he would be stripped bare of his clothes within seconds. The crowd resembled a hungry school of piranhas.

For the first time in his lengthy history with Pietro, Stefano questioned if his secretary was friend or foe. After all, his agreeing to stand upon the auction block like a slab of fresh meat had been Pietro's doing.

Stefano's gaze scanned the crowd until he found his secretary. His companion was standing against the wall with a short young woman, wearing a revealing dress that clearly made her uncomfortable. Each time Stefano glanced her way, she was nervously smoothing the full skirt, or adjusting the spaghetti-thin straps.

So this was Priscilla Rutherford. Stefano had learned everything he could about the young woman in the past several weeks. She was the only daughter of one of America's wealthiest men. As Pietro had assured him, she was a lovely creature, comely and pleasant to the eye. Priscilla Rutherford was a gentle soul who loved animals and children. She lived with her parents in their Lake Washington estate, and volunteered her time to a number of worthy charities.

The only drawback that Stefano could see was her domineering, manipulating mother who would like nothing better than to see her daughter marry well. It was unlikely that Elizabeth Rutherford would find fault with Stefano, but he wasn't looking forward to having a barracuda for a mother-in-law. A woman such as this could wreck havoc in his peaceful kingdom.

"I sincerely hope you're enjoying yourself, Your Highness," Madeline Marshall said as she curtsied deeply before him. She offered him her hand and Stefano bent forward at the waist and kissed her fingers.

"How can I not enjoy myself when I am with you?" he murmured. Madeline Marshall was another of life's small surprises. The woman was an eccentric, true, but she was a cagey business-woman who knew her product. And her product was romance. Madeline had earned his grudging respect with her organizational expertise and her leverage with the media.

Pietro had reported to Stefano earlier in the day that the autographing that was scheduled for Saturday afternoon had the potential for drawing in nearly eight thousand ardent romance readers. Stefano had been amazed, and had suggested to Madeline earlier in that evening that San Lorenzo would be the perfect location for a future conference. The tourist bureau would appreciate the plug.

"We've sold over thirteen thousand tickets," Madeline whispered to him, her eyes twinkling.

"I am honored that so many beautiful women are eager to spend an evening in my company," Stefano said with a graciousness that had been drilled into him from his youth.

"From what I understand, Priscilla Rutherford bought a thousand tickets. I don't mind telling you, I purchased a fair share of them myself," Madeline said with a short, nervous laugh.

"I would be most happy if I were to draw your name, Ms. Marshall," Stefano said, inclining his head toward her.

The businesswoman broke out in a sigh and pressed her hand over her heart. "If only I were ten years younger," she whispered. "I'd give you a run for your money."

Stefano didn't doubt the truth of that.

Sighing once more, Madeline asked, "Are you ready for the drawing?"

"Of course." As ready as any man could be who was about to face a firing squad.

Madeline Marshall stepped toward the podium. An excited hush fell over the crowd as a huge plastic barrel containing the entrants' names was wheeled onto the stage. Two muscular hotel employees stood guard at each side of the barrel.

"Ladies and gentlemen," Madeline said, commanding their attention. Not that the hungry crowd needed encouragement. "The time we've all been waiting for has finally arrived. Romance lovers have snatched up over thirteen thousand tickets, all seeking the once-in-a-lifetime chance to date Prince Stefano Giorgio Paolo, the Crown Prince of San Lorenzo—the world's most eligible bachelor."

An enthusiastic chatter circled the room. It seemed to Stefano that the group was pressing closer and closer to the stage.

"As I explained earlier," Madeline Marshall continued, "the winning ticket entitles the winner to an all-expense paid evening with Prince Stefano, at the restaurant of her choice. The monies collected for this evening's event have been donated to the Literacy Councils of King, Pierce and Kitsap Counties."

Applause followed. The two burly men edged closer to the barrel and energetically stirred the hopes and dreams of thirteen thousand women. The white entries tumbled one on top of the other.

When they'd finished, Madeline Marshall opened the trapdoor and motioned for him. "Prince Stefano, would you kindly do us the honor?" she asked.

Stefano nodded, stepped toward the plastic barrel and with a sigh, inserted his gloved hand. He burrowed his fingers through the entries, grabbed several and shook his hand until only one remained. He pulled that one out.

Stepping up to the podium, he looked out over the expectant faces of the women staring up at him. Priscilla Rutherford held her arms close to her breasts, her eyes closed and her fingers crossed. He wouldn't dare to hope he would draw the name of the woman he planned to make his wife. The Fates would never make it that easy.

He swore he could have heard a pin drop in the silence. He unfolded the slip, and mentally he reviewed the name.

"Hope Jordan." He spoke into the microphone.

A scream came from the back of the room as an older, gray-haired woman raised both hands. Stefano's gaze found her and he felt his heart drop to his knees.

He was about to go out on a date with a woman old enough to be his mother.

Two

"You won!" The nearly incoherent voice shouted into Hope's ear.

Hope propped open one eye and stared at the digital dial on her clock radio. It was nearly eleven. One arm dangled over the side of the bed and the other held the telephone receiver to her ear. The side of her face was flattened against the pillow.

"Who is this?"

"It's Lindy."

"For the love of heaven, why are you calling me in the middle of the night?"

"To tell you Prince Stefano drew your name."

Both Hope's eyes flew open. Scrambling into a sitting position, she brushed the hair from her face, pressing her hand against her forehead. "Why are you calling me instead of my mother?"

"Because when your name was announced, your mother screamed, threw her arms into the air and promptly fainted."

"Oh, my goodness—" Hope bounded to her feet and paced across the top of her mattress "—is Mom all right?"

"I think so. She keeps saying something about fate and Providence and the stars all being in the right place. The paramedics don't have a clue what she's talking about."

"The paramedics?"

"That's the other reason I phoned," Lindy announced. "They need you to answer a few questions."

"I'll be there as soon as I can," Hope

said, and in her rush nearly fell head-
first off her bed, forgetting where she
was standing. She swore she never
dressed so fast in her life, pulling on
jeans and a sweatshirt. She hopped
around the room on one foot like a jack-
rabbit in an effort to get on her tennis
shoes.

Driving into town, she happened to
catch a glimpse of her reflection in the
rearview mirror. And cringed. She must
have been sleeping hard because the
mattress had creased her cheek and the
hair on one side of her head resembled
a ski slope. Her deep blue eyes seemed
to have trouble focusing.

Hope left her car with the hotel valet
and rushed around the ambulance
parked by the entrance and hurried inside the lobby where Lindy was waiting
for her. Hope's appearance must have
taken her friend aback because Lindy
reached inside her purse and handed
Hope her comb.

"The prince is with your mother," she explained when Hope regarded the comb.

Hope had to stop and think what Lindy was telling her. "So?"

"I...I thought you might want to freshen up a little."

"Lindy, my mother fainted, the paramedics don't know what's wrong. I think Prince Stefano isn't going to care if I brushed my teeth."

"All right, all right. I wasn't thinking."

If meeting Prince Stefano was enough to cause her mother to require smelling salts, frankly Hope wasn't all that keen on being introduced.

Lindy led the way to the elevator, and they rode up to the eighteenth floor. Her mother's friends, Hazel, Gladys and Betty all rushed toward Hope when she stepped off the elevator. The three were all talking at once, telling her their version of what had happened after Prince Stefano read Hope's name.

"Your mother went terribly pale," Hazel said.

"I told you she wasn't getting enough carrot juice," Betty insisted. "She isn't juicing properly."

Gladys agreed. "This is the kind of thing that happens when you let yourself get irregular."

"She asked for you," Hazel said, ignoring the others, as she gripped Hope's arm. She opened the door to the room, and with an indignant sigh, said, "Those firemen wouldn't let us in. You tell your mother we're out here waiting for her." Hope started inside the room, when Hazel stopped her. "Tell Doris she can have the Hide-A-Bed if she wants."

"I will," Hope promised.

Hope found her mother sprawled across a davenport, the back of one hand pressed against her forehead. The other hand was being held by the most incredibly good-looking man she'd ever seen. If this was Prince Stefano, then no wonder her mother had fainted.

He was dressed in some kind of deep blue uniform with gold epaulets at the shoulders. A bright red banner crossed his chest, which was adorned with three rows of medals.

All at once Hope wished she'd heeded Lindy's suggestion about combing her hair. She looked a fright. Well, that couldn't be helped. It was too late to worry about it now.

Her mother moaned softly, and noticing Hope for the first time, Prince Stefano stood.

"Is that you, Hope?" Her mother's voice sounded as if it were coming from the bottom of a dry well. The question was followed by another low, breathy sigh-moan.

"Mom," Hope said, falling to her knees beside the sofa. "What happened?"

"I…I think I must have fainted."

"I'm wondering if you could answer a few questions?" a paramedic with a clipboard asked her.

"Of course." Hope reluctantly left her mother's side.

"There are just a few things we need to know," he said matter-of-factly.

Hope responded to a series of predictable questions, such as her mother's address, phone number, age. "As far as we can determine," the medic said when she'd finished supplying the information, "the fainting spell was caused by a sudden drop in blood pressure. Your mother seems to be doing fine for now, but she should check in with the family physician within the next week or two."

"I'll see that she does," Hope said.

The medic had her sign at the bottom of his report. "Do you have any questions?"

For one crazy moment, Hope toyed with the idea of asking if this fainting spell could be linked to a lack of carrot juice and irregularity. Fortunately, she stopped herself in the nick of time.

"Nothing, thank you," she said.

The medic tore the sheet from the top of the clipboard and handed it to her. Hope folded it in half and stuck it in the pocket of her acid-washed jeans. "Thank you for your trouble," she said, as the two paramedics gathered their equipment.

"Mom, let me take you home," Hope suggested gently, kneeling down at her mother's side.

Doris ignored the suggestion. Instead she tilted her head back so that she could get a better look at Prince Stefano. "Hope, this is Prince Stefano," Doris said, gazing at the prince as if he were a Roman god. Actually that assessment wasn't far off.

"I'm very pleased to make your acquaintance," Prince Stefano said politely.

"Me, too." She held out her hand, and

then, thinking this might be considered unladylike, quickly withdrew it.

The prince offered her his own hand just as she dropped hers. He dropped his, and she raised hers. Their eyes met and Hope saw a flash of amusement dance in his deep brown eyes.

"Prince..." Doris whispered, "please excuse how my daughter's dressed. She doesn't normally look...this bad."

Hope's face filled with color hot enough to fry eggs.

"Your daughter is as beautiful as her mother."

Doris released a languished sigh.

"I understand you and I will be dining together tomorrow evening," Prince Stefano said, smiling toward Hope. He was the picture of propriety and as stiff as cardboard.

"Do you like Chinese food?" Hope asked.

"Chinese food?" Her mother propelled herself off the davenport as if she were bounding off a trampoline. "You're dining with Prince Stefano Giorgio Paolo, not Gomer Pyle. We'll start off with cocktails at Matchabelles, followed by dinner at the Space Needle.... No," Doris corrected. "You won't have a moment's privacy there. The tourists will gawk at you every moment you're there."

Hope and Prince Stefano were left speechless by her mother's miraculous recovery.

"We must plan every detail," Doris said, her voice high and enthusiastic as she started pacing. "I'll need Hazel and the others to help me with this. You two leave everything to us, understand?"

"Ah..." Hope had yet to find her tongue.

"As you wish," Prince Stefano said, ever gracious. "I'm sure you and your friends will plan a lovely evening for your daughter and me."

Doris blushed with pleasure. "I promise you Hope won't look a thing like she does now."

"Mother!"

Prince Stefano's gaze briefly skirted past Hope's, and she caught a glimmer of amusement. He reached for her mother's hand, pressed his lips to it and said, "I'm pleased to see you're feeling better, Mrs. Jordan. If you need anything further, please don't hesitate to call either me or my assistant." He reached inside his pocket and handed her a small card.

"It was a pleasure to meet you," Hope mumbled, after finding her voice.

The prince smiled warmly. "The pleasure was all mine. I'll look forward to our evening together, Miss Jordan."

"I…I will, too."

It wasn't until after he'd left the room that Hope realized it was true.

Priscilla Rutherford stood, hiding out on the balcony, sipping from a champagne glass, and feeling mildly sorry for herself. She'd counted on winning the date with Prince Stefano. It would have been a dream come true to meet His Royal Highness. Priscilla was half in love with the handsome prince. The opportunity to meet him was the reason she'd signed up for the Romance Lovers' Convention. Now that didn't seem likely, although she wasn't sure what she'd say if they did meet. She'd probably embarrass them both by staring at him, too tongue-tied to speak.

The night was lovely with stars scattered like diamond dust across a black velvet sky. The honey-colored moon was full and seemed to be smiling down on her, or so she'd like to think.

Most people assumed Priscilla lived the perfect life. She was well educated, had traveled extensively and was heir to a vast fortune. But what she sought most seemed out of reach. She longed to be a wife and mother to a man who loved her for herself and not for her father's money.

She hungered for a simple life with a husband who hurried home at night to the meals she'd cooked herself. Mostly, Priscilla longed to be a mother. How different she was from her own ambitious one. It often puzzled her that she, who was so homey, could have been born to two highly motivated, sophisticated people.

The cocktail party was winding down, but Priscilla lingered, grateful for these few moments apart from the crowd. She enjoyed people, but often felt awkward and gauche when she was in a group of strangers.

Drinking the last of the champagne, she gazed out over the midnight-dark waters of Puget Sound. A foghorn from one of the ferries sounded in the distance.

"May I join you?"

Priscilla turned around to find a tall, dignified-looking man silhouetted against the bright light spilling from the doorway. She thought he might be part of the group traveling with the prince, but she wasn't sure. During the course of the evening, she'd seen him several times. Almost always he was in close proximity to her.

He was formidable in stature, muscular and nearly as good-looking as the prince himself.

"I...I was just leaving," Priscilla said shyly.

"Please don't," he said, joining her at the railing. Resting his forearms against the wrought iron, he gazed out over the city. "It's a lovely evening, isn't it?"

Priscilla detected a hint of an accent; otherwise his English was flawless.

"Very," she whispered. It would have been far more lovely if her name had been the one drawn by Prince Stefano.

"Are you terribly disappointed?" he turned and asked her unexpectedly.

She thought for a moment to pretend

she didn't know what he was talking about, then decided against it. Her disappointment was obvious. "A little."

He straightened. "Perhaps I should introduce myself. My name is Pietro. I'm the personal secretary to Prince Stefano."

"Pietro," she said, testing the name on her tongue. "You have just one name?"

He hesitated before answering. "Yes. The prince has six, and I've decided one is less confusing."

Priscilla smiled into the balmy night. "It certainly hasn't hurt Madonna any."

"No," he agreed amiably, "it hasn't."

Their silence was a companionable one. "Do you mind if I ask you a few questions about Prince Stefano?" She hoped she wasn't being impertinent.

"It would be my pleasure."

Self-conscious, Priscilla dropped her gaze. "Is the prince as charming as you are?"

"Much more so, I believe."

Priscilla turned and braced her back against the railing in an effort to better see this handsome, mysterious man. The moonlight beamed over his shoulder, illuminating his strong facial features. Prince Stefano was world-class handsome, but Pietro was no slouch in the looks department. "What's it like working with royalty? I mean, is it continual pomp and ceremony?"

"Not at all," Pietro assured her. "Naturally, there are a number of customary obligations the prince is required to attend, but I make sure his schedule is balanced with plenty of free time. The prince loves to ride. He's an excellent swordsman, and…"

"Swordsman? But who would dare to challenge the prince?"

Once again Pietro hesitated, and Priscilla could sense his amusement. "No one challenges the prince, Ms. Rutherford. Most often he's the one who offers the challenges."

"But whom does he fight?"

Pietro chuckled. "I'm afraid I'm his favorite opponent."

"Have you ever bested him?" Priscilla wasn't sure why she was so curious about Pietro's relationship with the prince, but the man fascinated her.

"We're evenly matched," Pietro explained.

"Then you've won?"

"On occasion."

Although everything she knew about Prince Stefano had come from gossip publications, Priscilla didn't think he'd take kindly to losing at anything. She'd only just met Pietro, but she had the unshakable impression that he wasn't a man who enjoyed losing, either.

"Have you ever *let* him win?"

"Never." His quick response assured her he was telling the truth.

"What's the prince like as a person?"

Pietro mulled over his response. "He's a gentleman. Generous to a fault. Sympathetic and sincere. He cares deeply for his country and his people."

"You make him sound like a saint."

Pietro cocked one eyebrow. "I hadn't finished yet."

"Sorry," she mumbled.

"He's not quick-tempered, but when he does become angry, it's best to find someplace to hide until he's worked out whatever is troubling him."

"My father's like that," Priscilla added thoughtfully, "but he's never angry for very long."

"Neither is Stefano."

"You're his friend, aren't you?" And just about everything else, Priscilla speculated.

Pietro didn't answer. Instead he surprised her with a question of his own. "Would you care to meet him?"

Her hands flew to her chest. "Is that possible? I mean, I understand he's only going to be in the area a few days and I wouldn't want to take up his time."

"Prince Stefano would deeply enjoy making your acquaintance." Pietro's voice was almost a monotone, crisp and businesslike, as if he were performing a necessary duty.

"I'd love to meet the prince. Every woman here would give their right arm for the opportunity." That she would actually have the chance was more than she could believe.

"He'd enjoy meeting you, as well."

"Me?"

"Why do you sound so surprised?" Pietro asked. "You're a lovely young woman."

It did her ego a world of good to hear Prince Stefano's personal secretary say such things to her. If only she weren't so clumsy and awkward.

"Tomorrow around ten for tea," Pietro suggested.

"So soon? I...I mean sure, anytime would be great."

Pietro removed a small card from inside his suit jacket along with a pen and scribbled the information down on the back. "I'll have the footman meet you in the lobby at ten. If you'll be kind enough to give him this card, he'll escort you to the prince's suites."

"Will you be there?"

It took Pietro a long time to answer. "I don't believe I will be."

"Oh," she whispered, unable to hold back her disappointment. He was about to leave when she stopped him.

"Pietro, after I show the footman the card, would it be all right if I asked for it back? I'd like to keep it as a souvenir."

"That would be fine."

"Good night, and thank you."

He squared his shoulders and bowed slightly before turning and walking back into the ballroom.

"You met her?" Stefano asked when Pietro joined him in the suite.

"Yes. Priscilla Rutherford's agreed to meet you tomorrow morning at ten for tea."

Stefano waited, and when his friend wasn't immediately forthcoming, he raised his hands imploringly. "Well, are you going to tell me about her, or keep me in suspense?"

"Her picture doesn't do her justice. She's beautiful."

Briefly Stefano wondered if they were discussing the same woman. The Priscilla Rutherford he'd seen from the stage was short and self-conscious. She looked like a timid soul who would run for cover the moment someone raised their voice at her. Not that it mattered. It wasn't her he was forced to marry, but her father's money. A bad taste filled his mouth at the thought.

"I could use a drink," he murmured.

"So could I." Pietro walked over to the wet bar, brought down two glasses, filled them with ice and poured them each a strong drink.

"How's the woman who fainted? What was her name...Charity, or something along those lines?" Pietro inquired. Stefano had the impression his friend didn't want to talk about the heiress, but then he was just as reluctant to mention Hope.

Stefano lowered his gaze to his drink, watching the ice cubes melt. "Her name's Hope. Hope Jordan. Actually the woman who screamed and then fainted is the mother of the young lady I'll be having dinner with tomorrow evening."

"You met her?"

"Yes. Briefly."

"And the mother?"

"She's fine...a little excited, but otherwise I'd say she made a complete recovery."

"And the daughter?"

"The daughter," Stefano repeated,

mentally reviewing his encounter with Hope. A smile tempted him. She had blue eyes that snapped like fire, and a look that could shuck oysters. Besides being completely incapable of disguising her feelings, the woman was downright impudent. Suggesting Chinese food... Damn, but he wished that was exactly what they could do. He'd like nothing better than to order out, then sit on the floor and use chopsticks while he learned about her life. Hope Jordan, despite her original hairstyle, interested him. Of course getting to know her beyond this one evening was impossible.

Even deep in thought Stefano could feel his secretary's scrutiny. "I'm sorry, Pietro. What was your question?" he asked.

"I asked about Hope Jordan."

"Ah, yes. We met."

"So I understand. What time's your dinner date?"

"I'm not sure," Stefano said. "Hope's

mother and her friends are making the arrangements. By the way, be sure and send flowers to Doris Jordan, Hope's mother. I believe she's staying at the hotel." He paused and thought about what he wanted to say on the card. "Tell her it isn't often a beautiful woman faints at my feet."

Pietro laughed, but grew serious once more. "Could you set a time that you'll return from your dinner date?"

"Why?"

"I was just thinking you might want to make arrangements to meet Priscilla for a drink afterward."

"No," he said adamantly, surprised by his own vehemence. "Ms. Jordan won a dinner date with me, and I don't want to cheat her by abruptly ending the evening in order to meet another woman."

"You're being unnecessarily generous with your time, aren't you?"

"Perhaps," Stefano agreed, but he didn't think so. He had the feeling he was going to enjoy Hope Jordan. It might be selfish of him to want to spend time with her, but frankly, he didn't care. A lifetime of getting to know Priscilla Rutherford stretched before him like a giant vacuum.

"Tell me more about the Rutherford woman."

Pietro's hesitation captured Stefano's attention. It wasn't often his friend was at a loss for words. "You don't like her?"

"Quite the contrary. She's delightful."

"But will she make me a good wife?"

"Yes," he answered stiffly. "She'll make you an excellent bride, an asset to the royal family. The people of San Lorenzo will be crazy about her."

"Excellent."

Pietro took a long, stiff taste of his drink, and then stood. "Is that all for this evening, or do you need me for anything more?"

Stefano was disappointed. He would

have preferred it if Pietro had stayed. Stefano was in the mood to talk, but he was unwilling to ask it of him.

"Go on to bed," Stefano advised.

"Will you be up much longer?"

"No," Stefano said, but he wondered exactly how long it would take him to fall asleep.

"Don't quit on me now, ladies," Doris pleaded, sitting Indian-style at the foot of the mattress. Her hair was confined to a cap and she wore a thick cotton bathrobe. "I told Hope and the prince that the four of us would make all the arrangements for their dinner date."

"Can't we do this in the morning?" Hazel asked, sounding like a whiny first grader. That was understandable, seeing that Hazel had taught first grade for nearly thirty years.

"I don't know about the rest of you, but I'm exhausted."

A chorus of agreement followed Gladys's announcement.

"I thought we were here for the Romance Lovers' Convention?" Betty muttered, her eyelids at half-mast.

Gladys lifted her head from beneath the pillow. "Just how much longer is that light going to be on anyway?"

Doris braced her hand against her ample hip. "What's wrong with the three of you?"

"I'm exhausted," Gladys repeated.

"It's barely midnight," Doris said, shocked by her friends. "How could you possibly be tired?"

Her question was answered with a chime of reasons that included a big dinner, cocktails and the excitement of meeting the prince.

"What was all this talk about renting a hotel room and being party animals?" Doris couldn't believe she was rooming with such deadbeats. "Wasn't it you, Betty, who claimed you wanted to call your son at three in the morning and tell him he had to come bail you out of jail?"

"Yes, but...I wasn't serious."

"Gladys," Doris said, eyeing her friend whose face was buried beneath a hotel pillow. "I thought you were going to stick your head out the window and serenade the prince."

The pillow elevated three inches in the direction of the ceiling. "The windows are sealed shut."

"Ladies, ladies," Doris tried once more. "We have work to do."

"We'll never agree...it's *hope*less," Hazel said. And thinking herself clever, she added, "No pun intended."

After debating for the better part of an hour, they hadn't gotten any further in planning Hope's evening with the prince than predinner drinks. From that point on, everyone had an opinion on where the couple should dine.

Hazel was partial to the restaurant

where she and Hank had celebrated their fiftieth wedding anniversary. But Betty seemed to think the prince might frown upon a steak house.

Gladys was sure Hope would be the one to object. "Would a woman who sells low-fat muffins eat red meat?"

"Can't we please decide this in the morning?"

"Oh, all right," Doris said. Her friends were a bitter disappointment to her. She reached over and turned out the light.

"Wouldn't it be something if Hope married the prince?" Betty asked with a romantic sigh into the stillness.

"It won't happen."

"Why won't it?" Doris insisted, chucking back the sheets.

"First off, men like Prince Stefano marry princesses and the like."

"Prince Rainier married Grace Kelly."

"That was in the fifties."

Silence fell over the room.

"Did Hope say anything when they met?" The question came from Betty.

"Not with words," Doris answered, "but a look came over her, like none I've ever seen. I tell you, ladies, it was like magic. I felt it. The prince felt it. It was like a bolt of electricity arced between them."

"You're not making this up, are you?"

"Either that or she's been reading too many romance novels again," Hazel inserted.

"I swear I'm not making this up," Doris insisted. "Prince Stefano didn't know what hit him."

Silence once more. Doris's eyes drifted closed. Someone sighed. Two more sighed collectively, and then...

"What about McCormick's?"

"We already decided against a steak house," Betty muttered.

"Yes, but they serve seafood, too, and I know someone there who owes me big-time. They can make sure this is an evening Prince Stefano and Hope will never forget."

The light switch was turned on, and Doris squinted.

"McCormick's," Hazel mused aloud. "Now there's a possibility."

Three

The following morning Priscilla waited in the hotel lobby. Her fingers repeatedly ran over the business card Pietro had given her the night before. The tall and stately footman arrived and read over the card without emotion when she handed it to him.

"Would it be all right if I kept it?" she asked. "I want it for my scrapbook."

He nodded briefly and returned it. Nervous, Priscilla held her breath as they approached the elevators. She'd dressed carefully for this meeting with the prince. Her mother had insisted on a white linen suit with a soft pink blouse, and a diamond brooch. It was something Elizabeth would have chosen to wear herself. If Priscilla could have had her own way, she would have picked a flower-speckled summer dress with a broad-brimmed white hat, but it would have been useless to argue. Besides, her mother paid far more attention to fashion trends than she ever did.

Both her parents were thrilled that Priscilla had been granted an audience with Prince Stefano. Although she was quick to assure them the invitation had come from a staff member, not the prince himself.

Priscilla feared they were putting far too much emphasis on a simple invitation to tea. Apparently they expected her to bowl the prince over with her wit and charm, and that just wasn't possible. She so hated to disappoint them.

"Could you do something for me?" Priscilla asked the footman as he inserted the special key into the elevator lock that would permit them entry onto the nineteenth floor.

"If I can," he said, looking mildly surprised.

"I need to talk to Pietro after my meeting with the prince. Would you tell him it's important? I promise I'll only take a few minutes of his time. I wouldn't disturb him if it wasn't necessary. Tell him that for me, if you would."

"I'll see to it right away."

"Thank you."

The elevator made a soft mechanical noise as it ascended. Priscilla's heart was close to blocking her air passage, and she worried about being able to speak normally when introduced to the prince. Her hands felt cold and clammy, and her knees seemed to be losing their starch. She couldn't remember being more nervous about anything.

The elevator doors smoothly glided

open and Priscilla was escorted into a plush suite that overlooked downtown Seattle and majestic Puget Sound. As always her gaze was captured by the beauty of the scenery.

"Your city is beautiful," the deep, male voice said from behind her.

As if caught doing something she shouldn't, Priscilla whirled around. Finding Prince Stefano standing there, she curtsied so low, her knee touched the thick wool carpet. The prince stepped forward, gripped her hand with his own and helped her upright.

The prince was even more dashing close up, Priscilla noted, and not nearly as frightening as she'd expected. She tried to remember the things Pietro had told her about His Highness. She tamed her fear by remembering he was a gallant gentleman who deeply loved his country. If she concentrated on the things she'd learned from Pietro, she might not worry so much about making a fool of herself.

"I'm pleased to make your acquaintance, Miss Rutherford," Prince Stefano said. "Pietro spoke fondly of you."

"I am very honored and pleased to meet you, Your Highness," Priscilla said through the constriction in her throat. "I appreciate your taking the time from your busy schedule to see me. I promise not to take up much of your morning."

"Nonsense. There's always time in my schedule to meet a beautiful and charming woman, such as yourself."

Priscilla blushed.

"Please sit down." The prince gestured to the pair of white leather wingback chairs.

"Thank you," Priscilla murmured, wondering just how long she'd be required to stay before she could speak with Pietro. "I have something for you," she said, taking the handwritten invitation from her mother and giving it to the prince.

He opened it, read the message and smiled. "I'd be honored to meet your family. Tell your parents they can expect me around three."

The prince engaged Priscilla in mundane conversation, and when there seemed to be nothing more to say, he carried the dialogue himself. He told her about the beauty of San Lorenzo, and invited her to visit his country at her earliest convenience, promising to show her the sights himself.

Forty-five minutes later, when it was time to leave, Priscilla stood gratefully and thanked him for his generous hospitality and the invitation to visit San Lorenzo.

The same footman who'd come for her earlier escorted her from the room. The minute they were out of earshot, Priscilla stopped. "Did you speak with Pietro?"

"Yes. He asked me to take you to his office."

"I hope I'm not interrupting anything important."

"He didn't say, miss." With that he led her down a wide hallway to a compact office.

"Please have a seat," he said. "Pietro will be with you momentarily." He closed the door when he left her alone. Priscilla sank into the cushioned chair, her knees giving out on her. She pressed her hand over her heart, closed her eyes and drew in a deep breath.

"Was it so terrifying meeting Prince Stefano?" Pietro asked from behind her, amusement woven through his words.

"Not exactly terrifying," she answered, straightening. "But I don't think I took a complete breath the entire time I was with him."

"What did you think?" Pietro walked around and sat down at a brightly polished desk across from her.

"Of the prince?" She hadn't had time to properly form an opinion, frightened as she was of making a mistake, or spilling her tea. "He's…a gentleman, just the way you said. He told me about San Lorenzo and invited me to visit, but I think he was just being polite."

"I'm sure he was sincere," Pietro countered.

"I've visited San Lorenzo twice before, but that was years and years ago. I didn't tell the prince that because I was far more comfortable letting him do the talking."

"You asked to see me?" Pietro asked.

"Yes." She noted that the prince's secretary was more reserved and aloof than he had been the night before. "I don't mean to make a nuisance of myself, but I thought I should explain about the invitation my parents sent." For forty-five minutes she'd sat with Prince Stefano and spoken no more than few words. Now, she couldn't seem to stop talking.

"My parents invited the prince to meet them tomorrow afternoon. I tried to explain to Mom and Dad that none of this would have happened if it hadn't been for you, but they wouldn't listen." They seemed to be under the delusion that she'd charmed the invitation from him herself.

"I'm sure Prince Stefano would enjoy meeting your family."

Dejected, Priscilla's shoulders drooped. This was exactly what she didn't want to hear.

Pietro hesitated. "Are you saying you'd prefer for the prince to decline?"

She nodded, feeling wretched.

"Is there any particular reason? Has Prince Stefano offended you?"

Her chin flew up. "Oh, no, he's wonderful. It's just that…well, if the prince comes, my parents might think he's romantically interested in me."

"If ticket sales for the date with the prince were any indication, this is what several thousand American women profess to want."

Priscilla didn't express her feelings for the prince one way or the other. She couldn't.

"If he meets my family, I'm afraid the prince might mention inviting me to San Lorenzo. You can bet my parents will jump on that."

"You don't wish to visit my country?"

"I love San Lorenzo. Who wouldn't?" This was going poorly. Every time she opened her mouth, she made matters worse.

"Then I don't understand the problem."

"No," she whispered, "you wouldn't."

"Tell me, Priscilla."

It was the first time she could remember him saying her name. Although his English was flawless, he said "Priscilla" in such a way that it sounded exotic and special. As if she were, herself.

"Are you free this afternoon?" she

found herself asking all at once, the words rushing together. "It would be a shame for you to be in Seattle and not see some of the city. I could show you Pike Place Market and we could ride the monorail over to Seattle Center." Priscilla had never been so forward with a man. She couldn't believe she was doing so now.

The expensive gold pen Pietro rolled between his palms slipped from his hand and dropped to the floor. Looking flustered, he bent down and retrieved it.

When he didn't answer her right away, she knew she'd committed a terrible faux pas. A man like Pietro, Prince Stefano's personal secretary and companion, didn't have time to spend with her. By blurting out the invitation she'd placed him in an impossible position. He couldn't refuse without offending her, and he couldn't accept, either. A man in his position didn't go sightseeing, and if he did, he wouldn't necessarily want to do so with her.

"Of course you can't.... Forgive me for asking. I wasn't thinking." She was far too embarrassed to meet his gaze. She stood abruptly, gripping her purse against her stomach. "If you'll excuse me, I'll..."

"Priscilla," he said in that gentle way of his, "sit down."

She was too miserable to do anything but comply. "I'm sorry," she whispered, hanging her head in shame.

"There's no reason to apologize."

She didn't contradict him, although she didn't agree.

"First tell me why you don't wish to accept the prince's invitation to visit our country."

She swallowed tightly. "It's because of my parents. They think there's a chance Prince Stefano will become enamored with me. They don't understand that he was just being polite."

"Your parents are the reason you'd prefer the prince refused their invitation for tomorrow afternoon, as well?"

She nodded. "I shouldn't have said anything, I know. It was tactless and rude of me. I was hoping..."

"Yes," Pietro urged, when she hesitated.

"He would decline."

Pietro sighed heavily. "I'm afraid that's impossible. Prince Stefano has already asked me to accept on his behalf."

"I see." So much for that.

"I don't think you should so readily discount yourself, Priscilla. The prince was quite taken with you. He told me himself what a beautiful woman he found you to be."

Priscilla blinked several times, uncertain if what she heard could possibly be true. "He told you that?"

"Yes. Why are you so surprised?"

"I just am."

"You shouldn't be. You're a beautiful person, Priscilla Rutherford." Pietro's smile was warm and gentle, and Priscilla felt mesmerized by it.

"Thank…you," she whispered.

Pietro's gaze abruptly left her, breaking the magical spell between them. "Prince Stefano will see you tomorrow at three," he said, becoming businesslike all at once.

"Will you be joining him?" She'd feel worlds better knowing Pietro would accompany the prince.

"No."

She signed heavily, and nodded. It would have been too much to hope for.

"Now…about your invitation."

Her gaze went expectantly to his. Their eyes met and held for a long moment. Priscilla didn't bother to disguise her wishes.

Pietro reluctantly dragged his eyes from hers, and it seemed to Priscilla that he found it difficult to speak. "I must decline, but having you ask is one of the greatest compliments of my life."

She managed a wobbly smile, hoping that he understood that if he'd accepted it would have been one of the greatest compliments of her life, as well.

Hope had never had anyone fuss over her more. Her mother and her mother's three softhearted friends had driven her crazy, going over every minute detail of her hair, her nails, makeup and outfit. The dress was made of black crepe that clung to her hips and looped down her spine, revealing nearly her entire flawless back. She'd never have chosen the dress on her own, but Betty knew somebody who knew somebody who owned the perfect dress.

The high heels were leftovers from her high school prom days. A bit snug, but doable for one short evening.

She dripped diamonds—not real, of course—from her wrists, neck and ears.

Between the four women, they'd come up with enough rhinestones to sink a gunboat.

The phone had been ringing since eight o'clock that morning. The *Seattle Times* asked for an exclusive interview following her date. Hope declined, but that didn't stop five other area newspapers from making a pitch.

How the media found out about her was beyond Hope. The last she'd heard, *Entertainment Tonight* had flown in a camera crew. On learning that, Hope appointed her mother as her official contact person, which kept Doris occupied most of the afternoon. It also gave her a feeling of importance to be the mother of the woman dating Prince Stefano. Doris ate up the attention.

"The limousine will be here any minute," Hazel said, checking her watch. "Are you ready?"

Hope didn't think she could be any readier. One thing was for certain, she'd never have agreed to all this priming if she hadn't personally met the prince the night before.

It wouldn't take much to improve on his first impression of her, that was sure. If the truth be known, she wanted to razzle-dazzle the man. This evening was a means of proving she didn't generally look like an escaped mental patient.

"The limo's here," Gladys shouted excitedly. She sounded like a sailor lost at sea sighting land.

Doris and the two other women rushed toward the window. Hope heard them collectively sigh. One would think Prince Stefano had come for Hope in a coach led by six perfectly matched white horses.

"Oh, my heavens," Betty breathed, gazing longingly out the window. "He's so handsome."

"I'll get the door," Doris announced,

as if being Hope's mother entitled her to that honor.

"You can't be out here," Hazel insisted, taking Hope by the hand, and leading her down the hallway to one of the bedrooms. "The prince might see you."

"He's taking me to dinner, Hazel. That's the reason he's coming to the house."

"I know. We just don't want him to see you right away. It wouldn't be proper."

"You're confused," Hope said, holding in a smile. "The bride is hidden from her groom until the last moment, not on the first date."

"I know that, dear, but this is a special first date, don't you think? We want to make an impression."

Since Hope was aiming for that goal herself, she allowed herself to be ushered from the room.

The doorbell chimed and she could

hear a flurry of activity taking place.
What her mother and Doris's three
friends were up to now, Hope could
only speculate.

Hope heard the prince and was
amazed at his patience with the older
women. They engaged him in a lengthy
conversation while they reviewed the
itinerary they'd so carefully planned for
the evening.

"Hope," her mother called, as if she
were wondering what was taking her
daughter so long.

Hearing her cue, Hope stepped into
the living room where Prince Stefano
stood waiting. Once more, her attention
was captured by the mere presence of
the man. He seemed to fill every inch
of space in the room.

Holding her breath, Hope's searching
gaze met his.

She wanted to impress him, wanted
to be sure he didn't regret that she'd
won this night with him. But she was

the one who felt as if someone had knocked her alongside of the head. Her lungs froze, and it was impossible to breathe. He was the most dynamic man she'd ever encountered.

Hope didn't believe in love at first sight. That was something reserved for romantics, for women with time on their hands, not hardworking coffee-shop owners.

This whole thing with winning a date with a prince had originally amused her. She found it incredulous that a woman would actually pay for the opportunity to date any man. Personally, she couldn't understand why someone would even want to date royalty.

All at once the answers were crystal clear, and she felt as if she were the most incredibly fortunate female alive. It was as though this evening would be the most important of her life. That this time, with this man, would forever change her.

Prince Stefano's eyes met hers and it felt as if every bit of oxygen from the vicinity had been sucked away. The prince was a man of the world, sophisticated and suave. He'd dated the most prominent, wealthy women on the continent, and yet when he gazed at her, he made her feel like a princess. His princess. She, in her borrowed dress, and rhinestone jewels.

"Miss Jordan, your beauty takes my breath away."

Hope's mother and her devoted friends each folded their hands as if they were praying and sighed audibly.

"Thank you," Hope murmured. It seemed such a mundane thing to say in light of the way seeing him affected her, but she suspected that her reaction wasn't unlike a thousand others.

"My car is waiting, if you're ready."

She reached for her evening bag, a bejeweled purse that had once belonged to Hazel's grandmother, kissed each of her fairy godmothers on the cheek and turned toward her prince.

Prince Stefano led her to the limousine. On the walkway, Hope heard the click of cameras, although she didn't see anyone taking pictures.

"The press has gotten inventive over the years," Stefano explained. "It wouldn't surprise me to find several hiding out in the trees. The press is something I've learned to live with over the years. Everything I say and do appears to interest them. I apologize if they trouble you, but I have little or no control over what they print."

"I understand."

"They're a nuisance, but unfortunately, necessary."

"I'm not concerned," Hope assured him. "I deal with all kinds of people every day at my coffee shop. People are people. It doesn't matter if they wear a camera around their neck. There's no need to be rude or unpleasant. The press has a job to do, and so do we."

"A job?" He cocked one thick eyebrow in question.

"You and I, Prince Stefano, are about to have a most enjoyable evening."

He smiled, and Hope had the impression it had been a good long while since he'd relaxed and enjoyed himself. A good long time since he'd last thrown back his head and laughed. Really laughed. Hope wanted to see that, if only so he'd remember her. And she definitely wanted him to fondly recall their time together.

The chauffeur opened the door, and Hope and the prince climbed into the backseat. The first thing Hope noticed was a bottle of champagne on ice, and two crystal flutes.

The prince's gaze followed hers. "The champagne is compliments of Madeline Marshall."

"The conference organizer… How thoughtful of her."

"The flowers are from me," he said, handing her a bouquet of a dozen long-stemmed red roses, tied with a white ribbon.

Hope cradled the flowers in her arms and buried her nose in their fragrance. It was the first time a man had given her a dozen roses, and she was deeply touched. "They're lovely."

"So are you." The words were whispered and it seemed to Hope that it surprised Prince Stefano to realize he'd said them aloud.

"From what I understand we'll be dining at McCormick's," Prince Stefano said next, recovering quickly.

"Yes. Hazel was the one who insisted we eat there. From what I understand, the food is delicious, but I think Mom and her friends were more interested in atmosphere." The four romantics were determined to do whatever was necessary to motivate the prince to fall in love with her, as if such a thing were possible. Hope had gone along with them because...well, because she'd met the prince by that time and was already half in love with him herself.

Once they arrived at the restaurant, the hostess greeted them warmly. Hope heard murmurs and whispers as they walked the full length of the restaurant to a private booth, separated from the other diners on three sides.

"Enjoy your dinner," the hostess said, handing them each oblong menus.

Prince Stefano set his aside. "From what I understand, our dinner has all been prearranged."

"You mean to say Mom ordered for us, as well."

"So it seems." No sooner had he spoken when a basket of warm bread was delivered to the table. The wine steward followed, bringing a bottle of chilled white wine for the prince to inspect.

Prince Stefano read over the label and approved the choice. The steward peeled off the seal and skillfully removed the cork. He filled the two wineglasses after Prince Stefano had sampled the wine and given his consent.

"I didn't dare to hope such a beautiful woman would hold the winning ticket," he said, saluting her with his glass. "To what shall we toast?"

"Romance," she said automatically.

Her choice appeared to trouble him because he frowned. Recovering, he nodded once and said, "To romance."

They touched the rims of their glasses and then Hope brought hers back to her lips. A feeling of sadness came over her all at once. She didn't understand how it was possible. Not when she was dining with the most eligible bachelor in the world, in an exclusive restaurant.

The newspapers had touted how fortunate she was, how lucky to have won a date with the prince. It dawned on her then that this sadness, this melancholy feeling came from Stefano.

She was about to ask him about it when the sound of a violin playing a hauntingly beautiful song caught her ear. A strolling musician came into view. He nodded as he played and lingered at their table. The music was poignant and bittersweet and swirled around them like an early-morning London fog.

"That was so beautiful," Hope whispered when the minstrel drifted away. Unexplained tears gathered at the edges of her eyes. She'd never heard the tune before, but it was compellingly sorrowful.

"You know the song?" Prince Stefano asked.

"No," Hope admitted.

"It is from my country. It's a story of a princess who fell deeply in love with a merchant's son. Her family has arranged for her to marry a nobleman and refuses to listen to her pleas. They forbid her to see the man she loves, insisting she follow through with the marriage contract."

"Don't tell me she kills herself," Hope pleaded. "I couldn't bear it."

"No," Stefano assured her softly. "The merchant's son knows that his love has only hurt his princess and so he leaves her, and travels to another country, never to return."

"What happens to the princess? Does she go through with the marriage? Oh, how could she make herself do it?"

"No, she never marries. Against her family's wishes she enters a convent and becomes the bride of the Church, forever treasuring the love she shared with the merchant's son in her heart."

"Oh, how sad."

"It is said their love for each other, however brief, was enough to carry them each through the rest of their lives."

"I...don't understand stories like that," Hope said suddenly. "They're so sad and so unnecessary. When two people love each other, truly love each other, there are no real obstacles."

The prince smiled sadly. "How naive you are, my beautiful Hope."

It seemed he was about to say something more when a plate of crab-stuffed mushrooms arrived. "I gather this is our appetizer," Stefano said, sounding grateful for the interruption.

They were enjoying their meal, a decadent assortment of meat and vegetables, when Hope first heard the rustle of voices outside their booth. She thought, for an instant, that she recognized her mother, but quickly discounted that. Doris had been adamant that Hope and the prince not be interrupted.

No sooner had the memory surfaced

than Hope heard a pitch like the one used by the church choir director.

"What was that?" Prince Stefano asked.

"I'm afraid to ask."

Sure enough it was her darling mother and company, who'd come to serenade the happy couple with a rendition of Henry Mancini love songs.

Hope grimaced and gritted her back teeth as they hit a discordant note in "Moon River." Listening to them was almost painful. Hope just happened to catch the prince's eye and they both just missed breaking into hysterical laughter.

When they'd finished the song, the prince had composed himself enough to slip out of the booth and politely applaud their efforts. He personally thanked each one. Doris grinned broadly and blew Hope a kiss on her way out of the restaurant.

"I'm so sorry," Hope said when the prince rejoined her.

"Your mother and her friends are…" He struggled for the right word.

"Hopeless romantics," Hope supplied.

"And you, Hope Jordan? Are you a romantic, as well?"

She wasn't sure how to answer him. Only a few days before she would have unconditionally declared herself a realist. Romance was for…those interested in such matters. She wasn't. She hadn't the time or the inclination.

Until now.

What a fool she was. If she was going to be this strongly attracted to a man, why, oh why, couldn't it be someone other than a prince? The likelihood of her ever seeing him beyond this lone night was improbable. This was Prince Stefano Giorgio Paolo of San Lorenzo after all.

They left the restaurant and discovered the limousine had been replaced by a horse-drawn carriage. Hope laughed out loud. "I swear they thought of everything," she said, looking to Prince Stefano. "Do you mind?"

"How could I object?" he asked.

With her slinky style of dress, Hope found it to be something of a task to climb onto the carriage. Prince Stefano gripped her waist and hoisted her upward, until her shoe found the footing.

His touch was gentle, and it seemed his hands lingered several seconds longer than actually necessary. Hope's heart rate accelerated substantially as he climbed into the carriage and settled next to her, instead of across from her as she'd suspected he would.

His arm circled her shoulders and he smiled down on her. "I think it's only fair that we live up to your mother's expectations for us this evening, don't you?"

"Of course," she agreed.

Seeing that they were settled, the

driver urged the horse forward. The carriage wheels clanked against the cobble road that stretched along the side streets leading to Seattle's waterfront.

The night couldn't have been more perfect.

Hope thought of a hundred things she wanted to say, and didn't voice any of them. The silence held a message of its own. For this one night, for this moment, words were unnecessary. It was as if she and the prince had known each other all their lives, as if they'd been intimate friends who knew each other's deepest secrets.

The prince brought her closer into his embrace and without her remembering exactly when or how, she found her head pressed against his shoulder.

Hope had never experienced anything like this. She closed her eyes, yearning to savor each moment, knowing they must last her a lifetime.

"How is it possible that I should find

you now?" the prince breathed at the ragged end of a sigh.

Hope didn't understand his question and twisted her head back in order to meet his eyes. They were filled with a bitter kind of sadness, the same bitter-sweet melancholy she'd sensed in him earlier that evening.

"I don't understand," Hope answered.

"You couldn't," he said, and breathed heavily. She brought her head back to his shoulder and felt his kiss against her crown.

Hope held her palm against his heart and heard the strong, even beat. His hand folded over hers as they left the waterfront and headed toward the hotel where the limousine awaited them.

Their night would soon be over, and Hope wanted it never to end.

By the time they arrived at the hotel, a small crowd had gathered. Prince Stefano climbed down from the carriage, and then expertly aided her. The lights were bright and there seemed to be a dozen cameras trained on them.

Whereas Prince Stefano had been tolerant and patient earlier, he was no longer. He shielded Hope as best he could from the glaring lights and hurried her toward the waiting limousine.

The car sped away at the earliest possible moment. The driver, without her having to give him her address, drove directly to her small rental house.

Prince Stefano reached for Hope's hand. "I shall remember and treasure this evening always."

"So will I," she told him, forcing herself to smile.

She didn't expect him to kiss her, but when he reached for her and brought his mouth to hers, it seemed natural and perfect.

Over the years, Hope had been kissed many times, but no man's touch had affected her as profoundly as the prince's. Hope's heart seemed to swell within her chest at the surge of emotion that overtook her.

She parted her lips to him and groaned when he deepened the contact. He couldn't seem to get enough of her, or her of him. By the time he broke away, they were both panting and breathless, clinging to each other as the only solid object in a world that had suddenly been knocked off its axis.

Stefano kissed her again and again with a growing urgency and then stopped abruptly, his shoulders heaving. His hands framed her face and his large, infinitely sad eyes delved into hers.

"I apologize."

"Don't, please." She clasped her hand around his wrist and brought his palm to her lips, kissing him there.

"I had to be sure…."

"Sure?" she questioned.

Stefano shook his head, and briefly closed his eyes. "Thank you for the most beautiful evening of my life." He paused, and she watched as his facial features tightened as if he were bracing himself for something. "Please understand and forgive me when I tell you I can never see you again."

Four

"Are you ready?"

Pietro's question interrupted Stefano's thoughts as he stood gazing out the huge picture window of the hotel suite. "Ready?" he turned and asked. He'd never felt less so.

"You're meeting with the Rutherfords in less than thirty minutes."

"Ah, yes." Dredging up some enthusiasm for this get-together with the heiress and her family was beyond him just then.

"The car is waiting."

Stefano turned away from the window. "Pietro, have you ever met some-one…a woman, and known from the very moment your eyes met hers that you were going to love her?"

"Your Highness," Pietro replied with ill patience. "If you don't leave now, you'll be late for your appointment."

Frankly, Stefano couldn't dredge up the energy to care. "Apparently you haven't experienced this phenomenon or you wouldn't be so quick to dismiss my question." Reluctantly, Stefano reached for his jacket and fastened the buttons with a decided lack of haste.

"What are the Rutherford names again?" he asked. Pietro must have told him a dozen times as it was. Stefano couldn't explain why they slipped from his memory, and then again he could.

Hope.

He hadn't been able to stop think-ing about her from the moment they'd parted. In the beginning, realizing how fruitless it all was, he'd resisted, but as the night wore on and morning approached, his ability to fight his feelings for her weakened considerably.

By early afternoon, he felt as though he'd been walking around in a cloud. Certainly that was where his head was. His heart, too. Dreaming impossible dreams. Seeking what he knew could never be. And yet...and yet, he couldn't make himself stop.

"James and Elizabeth Rutherford," his secretary replied.

"Ah, yes," Stefano said, silently repeating the two names several times over in an effort to remember them once and for all.

"As I understand, they're both anxious to make your acquaintance," Pietro added, following Stefano into the next room. "Speaking of Priscilla," he added, as though in afterthought, "have you given any consideration to your next meeting with the heiress?"

"No," Stefano stated honestly. "Should I?"

"Yes." The lone word flirted dangerously with insolence. "As I understand it, marrying her is the purpose of this entire journey," he added.

Stefano turned and his eyes searched those of his friend, wondering at the other man's strange mood. "As I recall she was the bride you chose for me."

"Yes," Pietro said with what sounded like regret. "I was the one who believed Priscilla would make you an excellent princess."

Try as he might, Stefano couldn't picture Priscilla Rutherford as his wife. It seemed a hundred years had passed in the past twenty-four hours since he'd first met the heiress. Stefano vaguely recalled the gist of his conversation with her, although as he remembered it, he'd done the majority of the talking. Every word she'd spoken, he'd been forced to coax out of her.

Stefano found Priscilla to be a gentle and likable soul. She'd been as nervous as a rabbit, fidgeting and discreetly glancing at her watch when she didn't think he'd notice. Once they knew each other better, and she learned to relax around him, Stefano was confident they'd make a compatible couple.

"I assume you plan to ask Priscilla to accompany you to the banquet this evening," Pietro said crisply.

"Ah, yes, the banquet." The Romance Lovers' Convention was ending the festivities with a lavish dinner affair—or so the brochures promised. Stefano was scheduled to speak briefly, but he hadn't given a thought to bringing a date.

"It would be a nice touch to invite Priscilla," Pietro suggested, "don't you think?"

Stefano nodded, making a mental note to remember to ask the heiress when he was with her later. He'd ask, because it was part and parcel of what needed to be done in order to save his country from financial ruin, but it was Hope he wanted at his side. He forced his thoughts away from Hope and made himself concentrate on Priscilla.

"Miss Rutherford's quite lovely, isn't she?" Stefano murmured more to himself than his friend.

Although a response wasn't required of his secretary, Stefano was surprised when Pietro didn't give one. He studied his companion, wondering at his friend's strange behavior of late. He might have said something, but his own conduct had been questionable.

Pietro crisply stepped across the carpet and held open the door for him. "As I explained earlier, the car's waiting."

"I want you to come with me," Stefano said, deciding all at once.

"Come with you?" Pietro repeated, as if he wasn't sure he'd heard correctly.

"Yes." Having said it, Stefano realized this was what he'd wanted from the first. "You can answer any questions Priscilla's parents might have while I talk with the young lady. I'll do as you suggest and invite her to the banquet. It might be awkward doing so in front of her family."

"I'd prefer not to go."

Stefano dismissed his companion's reluctance. "I want you with me, and be quick about it. We're going to be late."

Priscilla deeply loved her parents. She'd never understood how it happened that her gregarious parents had spawned a timid soul such as her. Personally, Priscilla would rather leap off a skyscraper than speak in public, yet her parents thrived on being the center of attention.

Priscilla also knew her parents deeply loved her, but she was realistic enough to know she was a painful disappointment to them both.

As a young girl, she'd striven to gain their approval, but as she matured, she realized she couldn't be anyone but herself. In theory it sounded quite simple, but often she felt like a salmon, fighting to swim upstream, battling the desire for their approval while struggling to be herself.

"Let me look at you, sweetheart," Elizabeth Rutherford insisted for the third time in fifteen minutes. "Now remember to square your shoulders. You don't want the prince to see you slouch."

"I'll remember." After three semesters in an exclusive charm school, Priscilla was intimately acquainted with all the ins and outs of etiquette.

"And please, Priscilla, you must smile. This is a joyous occasion." Her mother poked a finger in each of her cheeks, cocked her head to one side and grinned grotesquely. "The prince of San Lorenzo is coming to call on you."

"Mother, please. Prince Stefano is accepting your invitation. His visit has little or nothing to do with me." Priscilla didn't know why she argued. Just as she'd feared, her parents had her all but married to the prince. Little did that dear man realize what he'd done by agreeing to meet her family.

She'd tried to warn Pietro, but he hadn't listened. He didn't understand that her family viewed her meeting with the prince as something of a social coup. Nothing she said could make them believe that her time with Prince Stefano had come as a result of her meeting his secretary. Pietro had been the one who made all the arrangements.

Her parents had discounted that information from the very beginning. The prince, they told her, had sent Pietro to issue the invitation. A secretary did not make appointments without first conferring with his employer.

Their assertion seemed all but confirmed when Prince Stefano promptly accepted her family's invitation. The entire house had been in a flurry of activity ever since. The housekeeper had polished every piece of silver on the huge estate. Mrs. Daily, the cook, had been concocting delicacies for two days.

The staff had been with the family for years and this meeting with the prince gave them the opportunity to shine. And if their efforts prompted the prince to fall in love with Priscilla, then all the better. Everyone in the household glowed with pride that Priscilla had captured the attention of Prince Stefano.

At last everything was ready for the prince's arrival. Fresh flowers from the huge garden, Priscilla's first love, were beautifully arranged and graced nearly every room of the house.

Priscilla and her parents gathered in the formal living room, which was tastefully decorated in mauve and gray, and impatiently awaited the prince's arrival.

Priscilla couldn't remember ever seeing her mother this nervous. Even her unflappable father had seemed unusually tense. Every now and again, he'd smile at Priscilla and tell her how beautiful she was. In all her life, Priscilla couldn't remember her father saying such things. It seemed she'd waited all her life for a compliment from him and now that he'd given her one, she felt sick to her stomach with trepidation.

The doorbell chimed and Priscilla's parents exchanged looks as if they'd both been taken by complete surprise, and hadn't a clue as to who the visitor might be.

"I'm sure that's the prince," Priscilla said unnecessarily.

Her father cleared his throat and stood, his shoulders and back ramrod straight.

Silently Priscilla prayed that she wouldn't do anything to embarrass herself or her family. More than anything, she pleaded with the powers on high that once her parents met and talked to the prince, they'd understand that he wasn't romantically interested in her.

When she looked up, the first person she saw wasn't Prince Stefano as she suspected, but Pietro. His gaze briefly locked with hers and she knew within the space of a single breath that he didn't want to be there. She didn't share his sentiments. The moment she saw him, the room lit up with sunshine and her heart gladdened.

It would do her no good to explain to her parents that the prince's personal companion sent her pulse racing ten times faster than Prince Stefano.

Pietro diverted his attention away from her long enough for her to introduce him and the prince to her parents. After the pleasantries were exchanged, the five sat in the living room and sipped coffee and sampled a variety of delicate pastries.

Priscilla noticed that Prince Stefano and her father seemed to find a number of topics to discuss. They were deeply involved in conversation while her mother engaged Pietro in small talk. Although respectful, Pietro was clearly displeased to be thrust into this setting.

After a while, as she'd been instructed, Priscilla asked her guest if he'd enjoy seeing her garden. This was her mother's blatant effort to have the prince spend time alone with her.

To Priscilla's surprise and delight, Prince Stefano motioned toward his secretary. "Pietro's the one who appreciates gardens. I'm sure he'd be more than happy to see yours."

Priscilla cast her mother a plaintive look, when in reality it was all she could do not to leap to her feet and shout for joy.

She stood and watched as Pietro fiercely glared at the prince. Nevertheless he obediently followed her through the French doors. Once outside they walked down the winding brick walkway that curved its way through the lush, blooming flower beds.

Knowing he wasn't the least bit interested in viewing the garden, Priscilla led Pietro to the huge white gazebo that overlooked Lake Washington. A light, cool breeze came off the waters, ruffling her hair. Rainbow-colored spinnakers glided their way across the water, cutting a swatch of bright paint across the blue skyline.

"You can sit here and wait, if you prefer," she said politely.

"Wait?" he asked.

"I know you aren't interested in the garden. Why the prince insisted you come out with me, when it's so plain you had no desire to do so, I can only guess." It hurt to say it, but she braced herself and added, "I know you'd rather not spend time with me."

He was silent for a moment as though carefully weighing his words. "That's not necessarily true, Priscilla."

She loved the way he said her name, as if it were as pleasing to the tongue as the pastries they'd feasted on earlier. She closed her eyes wanting to savor the feeling.

"If you prefer, I can leave."

"Don't go," he said.

Priscilla swore those were the two most beautiful words she'd ever heard. Sitting inside the sun-dappled gazebo with Pietro at her side was a simple pleasure she hadn't anticipated in the events of this afternoon.

"I don't understand you," she said, studying Pietro. "Either you find me completely objectionable and deplore every minute you're forced to spend in my company, or…"

Pietro burst out laughing.

"Or," she said, smiling up at him, "you like me far more than you care to admit."

His laughter died as abruptly as it had erupted.

"Would you mind kissing me?" she asked him.

Pietro leapt off the bench and backed away from her as if she'd asked him to commit a heinous crime.

She laughed softly and shook her head. "Maybe kissing me would help you decide how you feel."

He paced the area in front of her like an escaped panther. His hands were buried deep inside his pockets, and he refused to look at her. "That won't be necessary."

Slowly Priscilla stood and planted herself directly in front of him. He was much taller than she was, at least six inches and she was forced to stand on the tips of her toes in order to meet his gaze. In an effort to maintain her balance, she braced her hands against his chest.

"Your pulse's pounding as hard as a freight train."

Pietro didn't comment, nor did he move away from her. His heart thudded hard and evenly beneath her palm. She watched a play of emotions work their way across his face as if he were involved in some great battle of will.

Encouraged by his lack of resistance, she closed her eyes and slid her arms upward until they were linked behind his neck. Then, with great care, she moved her lips over his.

The kiss was gentle, more of a meeting of the lips than anything deeply passionate.

When she'd finished, Priscilla blinked, lowered her arms and flattened her feet on the floor. It was then that Pietro eased her back into his arms. Holding herself perfectly still, the same way he had, she allowed him to kiss her.

Only it didn't stop with a mere brushing of their lips as it had when she'd instigated the contact. Pietro's kiss intensified until a slow heat began to build in the pit of her stomach and her legs felt as if they would no longer support her.

"Does that answer your question?" Pietro whispered against her temple.

She nodded, because speaking just then was beyond her. What he didn't seem to understand was that she wasn't the one with the questions. The answers had been clear to her from that first night on the balcony.

Pietro braced his forehead against hers. Several moments passed before he spoke. "I shouldn't have kissed you."

"But why? Oh, Pietro, don't you realize it's what I've wanted from the moment we met?"

He laughed softly, but he wasn't being sarcastic.

"I like it when you kiss me." She wrapped her arms about his torso and burrowed as deep into his embrace as possible, seeking a haven for the complex emotions brewing inside her.

"Priscilla, this is all very sweet, but unfortunately, you don't seem to understand. I don't mean to hurt you, but I don't share your feelings." The change in him came on as fast as an August squall. His hands gripped her upper arms.

Hurt and stunned, Priscilla voluntarily backed away. Her cheeks flared with color so hot, it felt as if her face were on fire. She'd misread him and the situation, and embarrassed them both by throwing herself at him.

The constriction in her throat moved up and down several times before she managed to speak. "I'm…terribly sorry." Pressing her hands to her fevered face, she added in a thin, pain-filled voice, "Please…accept my apology." With that she turned and ran to the house.

By the time she arrived at the patio just outside the garden, Priscilla's heart was pounding hard and fast and she was breathless. Taking a moment to compose herself, she was standing on the other side of the French doors when her mother unexpectedly appeared.

"I was about to come and search for you. Where's Pietro?"

For the life of her, Priscilla couldn't answer. Gratefully, she wasn't required to speak because the prince's secretary rounded the corner of the garden, his steps filled with purpose. He paused when he found Priscilla with her mother.

"I hope you enjoyed your tour of our garden," Elizabeth Rutherford said.

"It's delightful," Priscilla heard him answer.

She trained her eyes away from him and called upon a reserve of composure stored deep within her. Pride wouldn't allow her to reveal how his words had crushed her. In all her life, Priscilla had never been so brazen with a man. What he must think of her didn't bear considering.

With her pulse thundering in her ears, Priscilla walked back into the living room to find her father and the prince chatting as if they were long-time friends.

Priscilla sat back down and neatly folded her hands on her lap. Her father looked approvingly at her and smiled.

It was her mother who noticed something was wrong. "Are you feeling all right, Priscilla?" Elizabeth asked. "You look flushed."

"I'm fine." It amazed her she could lie so smoothly.

"I think it must be the excitement of having the prince visit," her father supplied eagerly.

For the first time since his arrival, Prince Stefano turned his attention to

Priscilla. "Did Pietro enjoy the garden?" he asked.

She opened her mouth to answer and discovered her throat had frozen shut. For an awkward moment there was silence.

"I found the gardens to be most pleasant," Pietro supplied for her. "Miss Rutherford is an engaging tour guide."

The heat in her face intensified tenfold.

"I realize this is short notice, Priscilla," the prince said, "but I'd consider it a great honor if you'd consent to accompany me to the Romance Lovers' banquet this evening."

Once again, Priscilla found herself struck dumb. The invitation couldn't have surprised her more.

"She'd be delighted," her mother supplied, glaring at her.

"I'd be...delighted," she echoed, her heart sinking all the way to her ankles.

This was exactly the thing her parents had been hoping to happen.

Priscilla found herself contemplating the prince. From the moment he'd arrived, he hadn't paid her as much as a whit of attention, and yet he sought her company. She could have sworn he was no more interested in her than the man in the moon.

Her gaze drifted involuntarily toward Pietro, and her heart clenched with an unexpected stab of regret. From the first she'd experienced an awkward fascination with the prince's companion. She'd believed he'd shared her feelings. Now she knew that not to be true.

Pietro wanted nothing to do with her.

"I can't stand this," Lindy cried after the last runner had left the coffee shop for his appointed rounds. She slumped into a chair and reached for a sugar-coated doughnut.

"Can't stand what?" Hope pried, although she was fairly certain she knew the answer.

"You've hardly said a word about your date with Prince Stefano. I asked you how it went, and you said great. Do you have a clue of how much that leaves to the imagination?"

"'Great' is a perfectly adequate description of our time together," Hope argued.

"See what I mean," Lindy cried. "You somehow manage to cleverly sidestep every other question. It just isn't fair."

"I had a fairy-tale date with a fairy-tale prince."

"Did he kiss you?"

"Lindy!" Hope flared, making busy-work at the counter.

Lindy grinned from ear to ear, and wiggled her eyebrows several times. "He must have, otherwise you wouldn't look so outraged."

"It isn't any of your business."

"Did you get to talk to John Tesh from *Entertainment Tonight*?"

"Yes, briefly." This interest the media gave her had been a nuisance.

"I bet you told them more than you did me."

Hope hadn't, but she doubted Lindy would believe her.

"Are you going to see the prince again?" That appeared to be the key question on everyone's mind.

A sadness melted over Hope's heart, and she shook her head. "No."

"Why not?" Lindy was indignant. "Aren't you good enough for him? It makes me downright angry to think that after all the trouble your mother and her friends went through to make you beautiful…"

Hope couldn't help it; she laughed outright.

Her friend frowned, not understanding what Hope had found so amusing. True, getting beautiful had indeed been a chore, but Hope would have willingly gone through ten times the effort if it meant she could be with Stefano again.

But that was impossible. He'd said so himself.

"It wasn't just your mother and her friends, either," Lindy continued. "You put a good deal of effort into the evening yourself. Aren't you the least bit upset?"

"The ticket entitled the lucky winner to one date with Prince Stefano. Nothing less and nothing more. I had my one date, and it was the most beautiful night of my life. Demanding more would be greedy."

"Is he everything the tabloids claim he is?"

Hope had read the articles herself. Prince Stefano was touted as being suave, gracious and gorgeous.

"He's much more." Hope couldn't make herself regret a single minute of her time with the prince. The memory of their one night together would last her a lifetime. Someday she would hold her grandchildren on her knee and tell them the story of her one magical date with a fairy-tale prince from a kingdom far away. What she would hold a secret for the rest of her life was how the prince had managed to steal her heart away.

"How's your mother taking the news you won't be seeing Prince Stefano again?"

Hope closed her eyes, knowing this would be difficult. "She doesn't know yet." Her mother and company had waited up half the night for a report. The four were so exhausted from all the planning and arranging that Hope could only guess that they were still asleep.

"Mom will understand," Hope said, and knew she was being unrealistically optimistic.

"When is Prince Stefano leaving Seattle?" Lindy asked next.

"I don't know. Soon, I suspect." But not too soon, her heart pleaded.

"What are you doing this evening?" Lindy asked, between bites. She dunked her doughnut into her coffee and then carried it to her mouth, leaving a trail of coffee en route. "I don't know why I'm eating this. I think it's because I'm so jealous."

"Of what?"

"You and Prince Stefano."

"Your prince will come," Hope assured her.

"Only mine will be disguised as a frog. Life isn't fair. I would have given my eyeteeth to have bought the winning ticket, and you didn't even care. Maybe that's my problem. I've got to stop caring."

Hope realized her friend was only half-serious. She saw the irony of the situation herself. Winning the date with Prince Stefano had been a fluke, but even so, it had forever marked her life. She couldn't shake the feeling that they'd been destined to meet, destined to fall in love and destined to never have more than a single night together.

"I'm going to read a romance novel," Hope announced with a good deal of ceremony. "You asked me what I planned to do this evening, and that's it." True, it was something of a comedown after the romantic night she'd spent with the prince. But it was a way of holding on to the memories of what she'd so recently experienced.

"At last," Lindy cried triumphantly. "To think it took a date with a prince to get you interested."

They talked for several minutes more and then the phone rang. The two women looked at each other and both knew it had to be Doris.

"At least she waited until the runners were gone this time," Lindy said, as Hope reached for the receiver.

Although her mother had heard

nearly every detail of Hope's evening with the prince the night before, Hope was forced to repeat them. Naturally, there were a number of places where she skipped the more private details.

"It's all so romantic," Doris whispered.

"Yes, Mother, it was."

"You like him, don't you, Hope?"

It took Hope a moment to answer, as if she were admitting to a wrong. "Yes, Mom, I do, but then I don't know anyone who could possibly dislike him. Stefano is a...prince."

Satisfied, her mother sighed.

It had taken nearly twenty minutes for Hope to extract herself from the conversation, and afterward, she found an excuse to work in the kitchen. Her thoughts and her heart were heavy.

No matter how hard she focused on the positive, it felt as if there were a giant hole inside her. It would take a very long time to fill. A very long time to forget. That was what made it all so difficult because she wanted to remember, but remembering produced pain.

She was standing in front of the automatic dishwasher, loading cups onto the tray before sliding it inside the washer for sterilization, when Lindy joined her.

"There's a man out front who wants to talk to you."

"I'm not in the mood to deal with any salesman. Talk to him for me, would you?"

"Nope." Lindy was wearing that Cheshire cat look of hers, grinning from ear to ear. "This person insists on speaking to you himself."

"I'm busy." Stopping the washer now was a hassle she wanted to avoid. It was bad enough to be indulging in this pity party without having to deal with some slick salesman who was keen on selling her coffee filters.

"Are you coming or not?" Lindy demanded.

"Not. If someone finds it so all important to speak to me, right this instant, when I'm in the middle of this mess, then you can tell them to come back here."

Lindy frowned, and then shook her head. "I don't think that's wise, my friend." There was a singsong quality to her voice as if she were just barely able to keep herself from breaking into peals of laughter.

"Being prudent has never been my trademark," Hope muttered.

"Do you want me to get his business card for you?"

Grumbling under her breath, Hope nodded. "If you insist."

"Oh, I most certainly do."

Lindy disappeared around the kitchen door and despite her melancholy mood, Hope's gaze followed her. From the way her friend was acting, one would think… Her thoughts came to a slow, grinding halt. Prince Stefano. Was it possible?

No. It couldn't be. Stefano had told her himself anything between them was futile. She'd viewed his regret, experienced her own.

Slowly, removing one yellow rubber glove at a time, she walked out from the kitchen, her eyes trained on the front of the coffee shop.

Her breath caught when she saw him, standing as stiff as a marble statue just inside the door.

Five

"What are you doing here?" The question was barely above a whisper. Hope was rooted to the spot, unable to do anything but gaze upon the prince in all his glory. He was even more devastatingly handsome and debonair than she remembered. Regal and noble all the way to his toes.

Prince Stefano smiled demurely and moved toward the counter. "I had an urge to sample your coffee," he said as he slipped onto a stool.

She didn't believe him for a moment, but had no choice but to pretend otherwise. "Would you like a latte?" It was difficult to keep the trembling out of her voice.

"That's the drink that's so popular in Seattle?"

Hope nodded. They'd briefly discussed her business, but she'd assumed his questions had only been polite inquiries. She hadn't realized he'd been paying such close attention.

Hope felt the sharp point of her friend's elbow in her ribs and assumed Lindy was waiting for an introduction. Hope didn't have the heart to tell her friend that she was meeting royalty with powdered sugar coating her lips.

"It sounds very much like café au lait."

"They're similar," Hope said and, looking to Lindy with her white lips, swallowed a smile. "This is Lindy Powell. She does all the baking."

"I'm pleased to meet you, Lindy."

"I'll get you one of my muffins," Lindy offered. "It's on the house."

The minute her friend was out of earshot, Hope leaned close to the counter. "I thought you said..."

His hand covered hers. "I know." He closed his eyes, and when he opened them again she saw a flicker of pain move in and out of his expression. "I came because I couldn't stay away. Last night...I couldn't sleep for thinking of you. I shouldn't be here. I'm afraid my selfishness will only hurt you."

"Having you stay away hurts me more," she whispered.

His hand tightened over hers. "Did you sleep?"

"No," she admitted reluctantly.

Her answer appeared to please him, because he broke into a wide grin. "Then you felt it, too?"

She nodded, unable to lie.

The door to the shop opened and Hope glanced up to find the windows crowded with several curious faces. Apparently the throng was hoping to catch a glimpse of Prince Stefano. Looking flustered, his bodyguard stepped inside the shop, safeguarding the door against intruders.

"We must leave, Your Highness," the beefy man said, looking concerned.

Stefano's mouth thinned, and he reluctantly nodded.

"So soon?" If anything was cruel, it would be Stefano reentering her life so briefly. All that held back the urge to beg him to stay was her pride.

"Meet me tonight," he whispered. "On the waterfront, inside the ferry terminal. You will be safe there?"

"Yes. But what time?"

"Ten…perhaps ten-thirty. I will come as soon as it is possible for me to get away."

Once more Hope's gaze was drawn to the growing multitude of onlookers, pressing against her shop window. She doubted that they'd have a moment's peace that evening once the prince was recognized.

"You'll be there?"

The wisdom of it was doubtful. She was setting herself up for a fall, but even knowing that, Hope found, she couldn't refuse him. "I'll be there," she promised.

He smiled then and it seemed the whole room brightened. He reached for her hand and gently kissed it, then abruptly turned away. The prince's bodyguard opened the door and with the aid of two footmen cleared a path to the waiting limousine. A commotion broke out once the prince appeared, and Hope heard several requests for autographs.

Within seconds Stefano was gone.

"He didn't wait for his muffin," Lindy complained, wandering to Hope's side.

"I know." Both of them stood immobilized, staring out the window as if they expected him to magically reappear. In a way that was exactly what Hope prayed would happen.

From the way Priscilla's family had reacted to the prince's dinner invitation, one would think he'd asked for her hand in marriage. The minute the prince was out the door, her parents clapped their hands with glee and hugged Priscilla.

"Mom…Dad, it's only a dinner date. Don't make more of it than there is," she pleaded on deaf ears. Her parents, however, were much too excited to listen to her protests.

"There's so much that needs to be done," her mother cried. "He'll be back to pick you up in—" she studied her diamond watch "—oh, my heavens, in less than three hours. Priscilla, come, we have a million things to do." On the way to the door, Elizabeth Rutherford barked orders to Mrs. Daily. When she realized Priscilla wasn't directly behind her, she returned to the living room and grabbed hold of Priscilla's arm.

Given no time to dissent, Priscilla was whisked off to an exclusive dress shop and forced to endure two hours of intense shopping. Her mother insisted her evening gown must be perfect, and after being subjected to at least fifty different ones, she hadn't the strength to object to the billowing chiffon creation her mother chose.

Personally, Priscilla thought she resembled Scarlett O'Hara without the nineteen-inch waist. She wasn't oblivious to her mother's choice. It was the dress that made her most resemble a princess, direct from the pages of a Grimm fairy tale.

Nothing was left to chance. By the time Prince Stefano arrived, she'd been pushed, prodded, pampered and prepared. Priscilla felt more like a French poodle than a grown woman.

The real problem was that her heart

wasn't in this dinner date. If she'd had her way, she would have escaped to her room, and curled up with a good novel. Burying herself in fantasy was the only means Priscilla knew would ease the ache left in her heart after her confrontation with Pietro.

Remembering what had happened inside the gazebo was enough to turn her cheeks to a brilliant shade of red. She prayed with all her being that somehow she would escape seeing Pietro that evening. Since he was almost always with the prince, she doubted that was possible.

The prince arrived promptly at seven, dressed in full military splendor. It amused her because other than the palace guards, she was fairly certain San Lorenzo didn't have an army.

His eyes brightened when he saw her. "I didn't think it was possible to improve on perfection," he said, taking her hand, and tucking it into the curve of his elbow. "My car is outside if you're ready."

"Have a good time," Priscilla's mother crowed.

The prince seemed preoccupied on the drive into downtown Seattle. She wondered at his silence, but didn't question it since she wasn't in a talkative mood herself. All she wanted was for this evening to be over with so she could go back to own life.

This entire business had taught her a valuable lesson: to be careful what you wish for. She'd wanted so desperately to win the date with Prince Stefano. It had seemed like such a fanciful thing to meet a prince. Now that she had, everything had gone wrong.

By the time the limousine delivered them to the hotel, the banquet was about to get under way. The prince escorted Priscilla to a table at the front of the ballroom, which put him in easy reach of the stage where he'd be making his speech.

They were soon joined by Madeline Marshall, her husband, another couple—and as Priscilla had known and dreaded, Pietro. Brief introductions were made, and the necessary small talk exchanged.

To her dismay, Priscilla was positioned between the prince and Pietro.

"Good evening, Priscilla," Pietro said softly, once they were seated.

"Good evening," she said, not looking at him.

What little appetite she possessed vanished. She picked at her salad, skipped the rolls and partook in polite conversation, all the while painfully conscious of Pietro's presence.

She felt the warmth of his body so close to her own. She smelled the scent of his aftershave, a spicy rum concoction that flirted with her senses. She struggled against the memory of his arms holding her close, of his breath against her face and the whisper of his kiss over her lips.

But the beauty of that moment had been forever destroyed. She wanted to erase his words, bury them under a romantic heart and pretend. But she couldn't.

In an effort to save her from making a bigger fool of herself, Pietro had been brutally honest, brutally clear. He didn't share her feelings. Nor did he welcome her attention. The embarrassment she'd suffered then felt more acute now as she sat next to him at the banquet, wishing she could be anyplace else in the world.

"There's something wrong with your dinner?" the prince asked, when she did little more than taste the prime rib. Others were raving over the meal, while she couldn't force down another bite.

"Oh, no, it's very good," she hurried to assure him. "I guess I'm not hungry."

Stefano studied her briefly. "Are you unwell?"

"I have a bit of a headache."

"Do you wish to return home?"

"Oh, no. Please, that won't be necessary. I'll be fine."

"An aspirin perhaps? I'll send Pietro for some." He glanced in his secretary's direction and she stopped him by placing her hand on his forearm.

"Thank you, but I have some in my purse."

The prince's attention flustered her. As for his offer to take her home, it had been more than tempting, but she didn't want to explain to her parents why she was back so early in the evening. They'd never believe she had a headache. And they were right. It wasn't her head that was troubling.

It was her heart.

When the program started, the others at the table relaxed and turned their chairs around in order to get a better view of the stage.

When the prince stepped forward to speak, Priscilla stiffened, not realizing how much she counted on him as a barrier between her and Pietro.

"You're not feeling well?" Pietro asked as the prince stepped onto the stage.

"I'm fine," she whispered, focusing her attention on the prince, not daring to meet Pietro's gaze.

The silence between them was as power-packed as a minefield. Every glance his way held the potential of exploding in her face. Conversation was unthinkable; she'd never be able to manage it without revealing her pain.

The prince's speech was short and effective. He spoke of romance and love, and claimed its strength transformed lives. Love had the power to change the world. His message seemed to come straight from his heart as if he were deeply in love himself.

Priscilla noticed that she had become the focus of attention, especially when the prince joined her once more. She was momentarily blinded by the flash of cameras. Apparently the press assumed she was the woman who had captured Prince Stefano's heart. She considered that almost ludicrous, but knew her parents would be ecstatic to have the speculation printed on the society page of the *Seattle Times*.

Following the programs and the award ceremony, Prince Stefano was surrounded by a handful of admirers, seeking an autograph or a moment of his attention. Priscilla stepped aside and patiently waited.

The prince looked apologetically her way, but she assured him with a smile that she didn't mind. Indeed if circumstances had been any different she might have been one of the throng herself.

"We need to talk." It was Pietro's voice that came to her, low and sullen.

Risking everything, she forced herself to turn and meet his eyes. Pain constricted at her heart. "It isn't necessary, Pietro. I understand. Really I do. If anything needs to be said, it's that I'm so terribly sorry for placing you in such an uncomfortable situation."

"You understand nothing," he said. His jaw was clenched and a muscle leapt in the side of his face.

"Perhaps not," she agreed, "but what does it matter? You and the prince will be gone in a few days, and it's unlikely we'll meet again."

"It matters."

Priscilla was saved the necessity of an answer when the prince motioned for his friend. Pietro immediately left her side, and returned a few minutes later, frowning.

"The prince has asked me to escort you home. It seems he's going to be tied up here for some time and he doesn't wish to detain you, seeing that you're not feeling well."

Priscilla's stomach knotted with relief that this evening was finally over. And with regret that the last portion of this night was to be spent with Pietro. "That won't be necessary," she said quickly in an effort to escape. "Really...I can catch a taxi."

"Nonsense. Neither the prince nor I would hear of such a thing. You'll come with me."

His tone brooked no argument, and knowing it would be a losing battle to argue further, she obediently followed him. He guided her out of the ballroom through a back entrance. She traipsed behind him as he wove his way around the kitchen staff. Several seemed to think Pietro was the prince, and stopped and whispered in awe.

To her surprise he didn't call for the limousine, but had the valet bring a compact sports car to a side entrance.

"What's this?" she asked. She was unwilling to sit in such close proximity to Pietro. At least she could put some space between the two of them in the limousine.

"A car," Pietro answered simply, while holding open the passenger door. Only moments earlier Pietro had sought her out, and now it seemed as if he would have given anything to avoid her company. Her pride had been badly wounded by this man once already. She didn't know if her heart was up to a second round.

"I appreciate the ride, but I'd prefer a cab." She ignored his protest, and raised her hand, hoping to attract the attention of a cabdriver on the street. Naturally, when she was desperate for one, the streets were bare.

"Priscilla, don't be ridiculous."

Standing on her tiptoes, she frantically waved her arm and called out, "Taxi!"

"Prince Stefano has asked me to personally escort you home," Pietro argued.

"Do you always do as the prince asks?" she challenged, walking into the middle of the street.

"Yes," he said bitterly. "Please allow me to take you home."

The gently coaxing quality of his words was what persuaded her to do as he asked. As the prince's right-hand man, Pietro was a man accustomed to issuing orders and having them obeyed without question. Yet he was willing to plead with her.

"Please," he said again.

Defeated, Priscilla lowered her arm and walked back to the curb. "All right," she breathed in an exercise in frustration.

"Thank you," Pietro murmured.

She walked back to the sports car and climbed into the front seat. The billowing skirt of her dress obliterated the view out the front window and she was forced to push it down. She felt like a jack-in-the-box who would spring out the minute her lid was opened.

Pietro joined her and had trouble locating the gearshift between the folds of chiffon. Priscilla pushed the fabric out of his way as best she could.

Pietro started the engine and when they stopped at a first light, he glanced at her. Priscilla felt his gaze, but couldn't see much of him because of her skirt.

She wasn't sure who started it, but soon they were both consumed with laughter. For safety's sake, Pietro pulled over to the curb. Soon their merriment died down, and there was silence.

"You are a beautiful woman," Pietro said with all sincerity, "but this dress is wrong for you."

Priscilla had known it the moment she'd tried it on. Her mother had attempted to dress her in a way that would prove to the prince she would make him an ideal wife.

"I've offended you?" he asked.

"No," she assured him.

He waited a moment and Priscilla assumed he was going to say something more, but she was wrong. When traffic cleared, he eased the car back into the flow.

More at ease with him now, Priscilla relaxed. "You…you said you wanted to talk to me," she reminded him. Now was as good a time as any.

Once again he hesitated. "Not now."

She hated that imperious way he spoke, as if everything were on his terms, on his time. "Why not?" she demanded.

"Because I'm angry."

"With me?"

"No…no." His tone gentled considerably. "Never with you, Priscilla. Never with you."

She wouldn't be so easily appeased this time. This man confused and frustrated her. "Then who?"

He waited for several seconds, then said, "Prince Stefano."

His answer surprised her. "But why?"

"You wouldn't understand."

"I might."

"No, my love. It's complicated and best left unsaid."

His love. Only that afternoon he'd pushed her out of his arms and left her reeling with shock and embarrassment. Now he was speaking to her in the tenderest of endearments.

Unwilling to be hurt again, Priscilla gathered her pride about her like a shawl and slowly drew inside herself.

Other than the hum of the engine, there was no sound. The void seemed to stretch and expand, like yeast in bread dough. She felt Pietro's gaze studying her in the dark.

"Don't be angry with me," he implored. "I can't bear that."

"Then don't call me your love," she returned heatedly. Her voice quivered, making it sound as if she were close to breaking into tears.

Her words were met with stark silence, as if she'd shocked him. At the first opportunity, Pietro pulled off to the side of the road. He sat with his hands braced against the steering wheel, and after a moment a deep sigh rumbled through his chest.

"I'm going to kiss you, Priscilla."

She blinked, uncertain she'd heard him correctly. "Kiss me?" He made it sound as if this were the last thing he wanted. "But why…?"

"I don't think I can keep from kissing you."

"But you said earlier that…"

"Forget what I said for now." He

turned off the engine and turned toward her. Their gazes met in the dim light and locked hungrily. "Forget everything I said this afternoon."

Slowly he lowered his mouth to hers.

Priscilla wanted to turn away from him, if for nothing more than to salvage her pride, but she couldn't summon even a token resistance. The moment his lips touched hers, she realized that being in Pietro's arms was more important than anything.

Hope sat with her hands buried deep in her windbreaker on the hard wooden bench inside the ferry terminal. She'd been waiting nearly twenty minutes and Stefano still hadn't shown. By all that was right she should be home and in bed asleep.

The sound of heavy footsteps echoed against the hard floor. Her heart leapt with anticipation and she looked up, and saw that it wasn't the prince. She couldn't quite believe it, but whoever it was, resembled Elvis.

Her shoulders sagged with disappointment, and she buried her chin against her chest. She was a fool. No one else would have waited this long. No one else would have gone on hoping he'd come when it was clear he wasn't going to show.

"Hope."

Her head shot up, and she frowned. The man standing before her was Elvis and yet...

"Stefano?"

He grinned and, breathing heavily, he sat down next to her. "I fooled you?"

"Yes." She couldn't keep the amusement out of her voice or her eyes. She'd looked directly at him and hadn't realized it was Stefano. He wore a pair of rhinestone-studded white bell-bottoms and matching top, and a white scarf was draped around his neck. "What have you done to yourself?"

"I needed to escape the hotel without being noticed."

"In that outfit?"

He laughed. "Don't scoff. I paid good money for this costume."

"Where in the name of heaven did you get it?"

"From the Elvis impersonator who's performing in the cocktail lounge." He was only now catching his breath. "I can't believe you're still here. I was afraid you'd left, but I found it impossible to slip away unnoticed."

"But why?" That was by far the more curious of her questions.

The laughter drained from his eyes. "So I could be alone with you. If I came as myself, we'd be interrupted constantly. I am being selfish, but I don't wish to share this time with anyone but you."

If that was being greedy, then she was guilty, as well.

"Come," he said, standing and reaching for her hand.

"Where are we going?"

The question seemed to catch him unaware. "I don't know yet. It is enough that we are together."

They walked down the ramp out of the ferry terminal and onto the sidewalk. Although it was almost eleven o'clock, the streets were filled with the continual flow of foot traffic.

Stefano slipped his arm around her waist and they strolled together. Stefano seemed unconcerned with the attention his disguise attracted. Every now and again someone would shout, "Hello, Elvis," and he'd give a friendly wave.

Finally Stefano turned off the sidewalk and led her down a long pier lined with tourist and art shops. They stopped at the end and looked out over the deep, dark waters.

The night was gorgeous and the lights from West Seattle and the smaller islands of Puget Sound glowed like rows of bright bulbs on a Christmas tree.

Stefano turned Hope into his embrace and locked his hands at the small of her back. Sighing softly, she found a peace, a serenity she couldn't explain.

Stefano kissed her cheek, her ear, her hair, before claiming her mouth. Hope experienced a deep, almost painful longing. The prince trembled and she knew he was as deeply affected by their kisses as she.

Hope pressed her head against his shoulder and closed her eyes as the warm sensations melted over her. Biting into her lower lip, she tried not to think of the impossibility of their situation.

"I was afraid of that," Stefano murmured against her hair.

"Of what?" she asked.

"Your kiss. It's even better than before." His words were sad, almost bitter, and she lifted her head, wanting to look into his eyes. He wouldn't let her.

"Please," he said gently, "let me hold you a little longer."

Hope hadn't the strength of will to resist him. Nestled in his arms, it seemed as if the world and all the troubles that plagued the universe were a million miles away.

"When I was a little girl, I used to dream of meeting a handsome prince," she told him, finding life ironic. "My mother would read me a story before I went to sleep and she'd kiss me goodnight and then tell me that someday my prince would come."

"Ah, yes, your mother." Amusement laced his words. A moment passed and he chuckled softly.

Hope's head sprang upward. "What's she done now?"

"Nothing," he said, pressing her head back to his shoulder. "Don't be so concerned."

"Stefano, I know my mother. Please tell me what she's up to this time."

He chuckled softly and brushed his lips against hers. "I received a letter from her this afternoon."

"And…" Hope coaxed.

"She wanted to know what my intentions toward you were."

"No." Mortified, Hope buried her face in his chest. "I apologize…. Oh, Stefano, forgive her. She means no harm. It's just that…" Try as she might, Hope didn't have a prayer of explaining, because she didn't have a hope of analyzing what her mother could have been thinking. "It's just that…"

"Perhaps she believes I'm the prince she told you was coming all these years."

"Mom and her friends are romantics," Hope offered as a possible explanation. "They don't understand that life isn't filled with happy endings."

It seemed his hold on her tightened

briefly. "Let's not speak of the future. Not tonight. It is selfish to indulge myself with you, I know, but it is a little thing, and I hope in time you'll find it in your heart to forgive me."

Hope didn't want to think of the future, either. It went without saying she wouldn't—couldn't be—part of his life. Like Stefano, she was content to indulge her fantasies.

They didn't seem to have a lot to say. Together they sat on a bench at the end of the pier and he wrapped his arm around her shoulder. Every now and again he'd kiss her. In the beginning his kisses were gentle, but they soon took on an intensity that left Hope breathless.

He stopped abruptly and brushed a strand of hair from her cheek, and his hand lingered there. Several moments passed before he gave in to the temptation and kissed her again. She parted her lips to him and his tongue sought hers, involving her in a slow, erotic game.

Hope's breathing became heavy and shallow and when he raised his head, his gaze sought hers in the moonlight. She noted that his eyes were dark with passion and knew her own were a reflection of his.

His mouth found hers once more and when he dragged his lips away, he pressed his forehead to hers. "I can't kiss you again," he whispered.

The funny thing with greed, Hope discovered, was that she was never satisfied. At one time all she wanted was to spend time with him, then she'd be happy, she told herself. Then he kissed her, and she never wanted it to end.

"Why can't you kiss me?" she asked, spreading a series of kisses over his face, starting at his jaw and working her way over the contour of his face, teasing his lips with the tip of her tongue.

"Hope..." He trapped her face between his hands.

"Hmm?"

He directed her mouth to his and it was as if they were reuniting after a six-month absence. When he pulled away, Hope saw that his face was tight with desire.

"We must stop," he murmured, sounding very much as if he were in pain.

"I know...but I'm greedy for you."

"That's the problem," he murmured. "I am greedy for you, too. I just didn't know..."

"Didn't know what?"

"How much I need you," he whispered. "Now, please, don't tempt me anymore. You make me weak and—" he chuckled softly "—strong."

"That makes no sense."

"I know, but it's the truth." He pressed her fingers to his lips. "I want you to tell me more of your childhood."

"But, Stefano, I'm so...ordinary. Tell me of yours."

"I have no interest in hearing myself speak. Tell me everything there is to know about you."

"What about my old boyfriends? Do you want to hear about them, as well?"

"No," he said and laughed softly. "It wouldn't take very much to make me insanely jealous."

"It would only be fair," she chided. "I've been reading about your exploits for years. You aren't called the Bachelor Prince for nothing." She meant to tease him, to make light of his reputation.

He surprised her by clasping her upper arms. His eyes locked with her.

"It's true, there've been many women in my life."

"I know." She lowered her gaze, not wanting to think about all the beautiful females who had loved him. And worse. Whom he'd loved.

He lifted her chin with his index finger. "But there's only been one woman who held my heart in the palm of her hand." He reached for her hand and kissed her palm. "That woman, Hope Jordan, is you."

Six

It was the wee hours of the morning before Stefano returned to the hotel. He couldn't remember a time in his life that he'd been happier.

All his life he'd been groomed for his position as the Prince of San Lorenzo. He'd been taught the concerns of his country must come first. Duty and sacrifice were equated with honor and character. He knew he must marry Priscilla Rutherford or some other woman who was equally wealthy. There was no other option.

Now certainly wasn't the time to fall

in love. Now wasn't the time to give his heart to a woman he must eventually leave.

A week, he told himself. He would give himself that time with Hope as a gift. Seven days would be ample time to fill his heart with memories. Ones that he would need to last him a lifetime.

He'd been honest with Hope from the first. She understood and accepted that there could be no future for them. And yet she'd generously opened her heart and her life to him.

By the time Stefano let himself into his suite, he realized how exhausted he was, and yet he doubted that he'd sleep. Sleep would rob him of the precious moments he had to think about Hope, to remember the taste of her kisses and how right it felt to hold her in his arms.

"Where have you been?"

Pietro's hard voice rocked Stefano. Never had anyone dared to speak to him in such a tone.

"Pietro?" His friend stood by the picture window, his hands clasped behind his back as if he'd been furiously pacing. "Is something wrong?"

"Only that you'd disappeared!" he snapped. Walking over to the phone, Pietro punched out a series of numbers and spoke brusquely to James, Stefano's bodyguard, reporting the prince's safe return.

"I apologize, my friend. I wasn't thinking."

"What is this…this ridiculous outfit?" Pietro gestured toward the Elvis costume as if he found it distasteful to look at.

"What does it look like?" Stefano was prepared to give his secretary a little slack, but Pietro was stepping dangerously close to his limit. As the crown prince, he rarely had to account for his actions, and certainly not for his choice of wardrobe.

"It looks like you've been making a fool of yourself," Pietro said heatedly.

"Pietro," Stefano barked. "I think it would be better if we saved this conversation for morning. I've already apologized for any dismay I may have caused you and the others. It's late and you're upset."

"I'm more than upset." His secretary walked over to the desk and reached for a typewritten sheet, jerking it off the top with enough energy to send several papers fluttering to the floor. He ignored the disruption and slapped the single page down on the table next to where Stefano was standing.

"This is my letter of resignation, effective immediately." Having made that announcement, Pietro stormed over to the window and stood with his back to Stefano.

The prince couldn't have been more surprised if his secretary and friend had pulled a gun on him. The betrayal was as shocking.

Stefano sank onto the sofa cushions, hardly able to believe what he was reading. Pietro had been with him for years. He was far more than his secretary and companion. Pietro was his friend. The best he'd ever had.

"Is there a reason for your resignation, other than my tardiness this evening?" he managed to ask after a strained moment.

Pietro whirled around to face him. Their gazes locked in a fierce battle of wills. It felt as if they breathed simultaneously, each harboring his own grief.

"Yes," Pietro admitted reluctantly.

"You are free to tell me what I've done to offend you." He wanted this confrontation to be man-to-man, not prince to subject, not employer to employee.

Pietro chose to sit in the chair across from him. His friend was a large man, and when he leaned forward their knees almost touched.

"I cannot. I will not," he amended heatedly, "allow you to treat Priscilla Rutherford in such an insulting manner. She is a woman worthy of being your bride."

"I fully intend to marry the woman," Stefano argued, but he could see that his reassurances did little to appease Pietro. "That's what you want, isn't it?" Stefano asked.

"Yes," he barked. "But give me one good reason she would want you after the horrible way you've treated her."

Stefano didn't have a clue what Pietro was speaking about. "Forgive me for being obtuse, but what terrible sin have I committed against the woman?"

It didn't take Pietro long to answer.

"First off, you visit her home and meet her family and completely ignore Priscilla."

Now that Pietro mentioned it, Stefano did recall becoming heavily involved in a conversation with James Rutherford. He'd been distracted, but as he remembered it, Priscilla hadn't seemed to mind.

"Nor can there be any excuse for this evening," Pietro continued.

"This evening at the banquet?" Stefano had thought he'd been attentive and thoughtful. It was apparent from the beginning that Priscilla had been ill. Rather than detain her while he dealt with the many women who sought an audience, he'd had Pietro escort her home.

"I never intended to insult her. I assumed she wasn't feeling well and thought to see to her comfort as quickly as possible."

True, he'd been eager to escape the banquet so he could meet Hope, but that had nothing to do with his time with Priscilla. "First thing in the morning, I'll send flowers and beg her indulgence," Stefano offered, hoping that would appease his secretary.

Pietro rubbed a hand down his face, and Stefano couldn't remember seeing his friend look more tired. "I've already seen to that."

"Thank you," Stefano murmured, inclining his head.

Pietro clenched his hands over his knees. "Answer me one thing."

"Of course."

"Do you care for Priscilla?"

If asked if he loved her, Stefano would have been honest. He liked Priscilla Rutherford, and was comfortable enough with her that in time he was confident he would grow to feel a deep tenderness for her. "Yes, I care for her."

"Then you intend to marry her?"

Stefano had no option. Pietro knew that better than anyone. "If she agrees to be my bride, then we will be married at the first opportunity."

Pietro lowered his gaze and after a long moment, said, "Good."

"My hope is that once we return to San Lorenzo, she will follow with her family. Once she stays at the palace and samples what her life would be like there, I'll court her seriously." He hesitated, wondering if the heiress had said something to Pietro that he should know. "Do you know what her feelings are toward me?"

"No," came the stark answer.

Stefano waited a moment more, and tore Pietro's letter of resignation in half. "Now, can we forget this nonsense? It's late and we're both tired."

Pietro studied the torn piece of paper. "I will stay with you until we return to San Lorenzo," he said, his look both troubled and thoughtful. "If you want, I'll interview the applicants for my replacement, and leave as soon as one can be trained."

Stunned, Stefano nodded. "As you wish."

Stefano woke with a heavy heart. Unfortunately, the morning didn't bring any better news. He dressed, and when his breakfast arrived, he sat alone at the table and sipped his first cup of coffee. From habit, he reached for the morning newspaper, and scanned the headlines. As he reached for a baguette, his gaze fell upon the society page. The image of his own face smiled up to benignly greet him. It wasn't as though he were unaccustomed to finding his picture in the paper. Cameras routinely followed him.

But this photograph was different because Priscilla Rutherford was standing next to him. The lens had caught them at an opportune moment in which they happened to be gazing at each other.

For all intents and purposes it looked as if they were deeply in love. The headlines gave way to speculation that an American had laid claim to Prince Stefano's heart.

The speculation in the article was even worse. The more he read, the more alarmed Stefano became. The entire piece was geared toward Stefano's attention to the heiress, and speculation as to where the romance would lead.

Stefano feared Hope would read this article and think terrible things of him. He must talk to her, assure her he wasn't playing her for a fool. But just as he reached for the telephone, Pietro brought him in some documents that required his signature.

Stefano didn't dare risk contacting Hope with Pietro in the room. As much as it was possible, he wanted to keep his relationship with Hope a secret. Later, when it became necessary for him to leave, he wanted to spare her any unnecessary attention, and/or embarrassment.

His only opportunity to speak privately with Hope was to find some errand on which to send Pietro. "I need you to do something for me at your earliest convenience," Stefano said, reaching for his gold pen and a monogrammed sheet of paper.

"Of course," Pietro replied stiffly.

Stefano wrote out a message as quickly as his hand would move the pen. He folded the note and inserted it inside an envelope. "Personally deliver this to Miss Rutherford for me," he said, "and await her response."

Pietro hesitated long enough to attract Stefano's attention. "Would you like me to leave right away?" Pietro asked.

"Please," Stefano said. He didn't know what was wrong with Pietro, but his tone implied that he'd rather walk off a gangplank than carry out this errand. If he wasn't so anxious to speak to Hope, he would have questioned his friend.

Pietro reluctantly accepted the envelope. Stefano waited until his secretary had left the room before reaching for the telephone. An eternity passed before the first ring. A second, third and a fourth followed before her answering machine clicked on.

He listened to Hope's voice and even though it came through a mechanical device, Stefano's spirits lifted just hearing her speak. She sounded upbeat and energetic, giving instructions to wait for the long beep.

"Hope, my princess..." Stefano hated machines. Now that he could speak, he didn't know what to say. "Please, my darling, don't be influenced by anything you read in the papers. You own my heart. Meet me this evening as we arranged. It's vital that we speak." With that he replaced the telephone receiver, convinced his message was grossly inadequate.

He covered his face with his hand and sighed heavily. If she hadn't already read the article, she would now. With one phone call he might have destroyed his relationship with the only woman he'd ever loved.

Priscilla endured breakfast with her parents while they touted the virtues of Prince Stefano as if he were a god. As far as either of them were concerned, the man was perfect in every way.

Neither bothered to ask about her evening. Apparently they assumed everything had been wonderful from beginning to end. But then Priscilla hadn't volunteered any information, either, and if the truth be known, she didn't know what she'd say if they asked.

The fever pitch accelerated when her mother read the morning paper and found Priscilla pictured with the prince taking up almost half of the society page.

By midmorning, the phone was ringing off the hook, and Elizabeth was in heaven delivering tidbits of speculation to her dearest friends.

As soon as she was able, Priscilla escaped with a book to the gazebo, one of her favorite hiding places. Her intention was to bury herself in the carefree world of a good story, but try as she might to concentrate, her attention repeatedly wandered from the printed page.

Instead of becoming absorbed in the novel, her thoughts countlessly reviewed the time she'd spent with Pietro. The man confused her more than anyone she'd ever known. But it didn't stop there. He intrigued her, as well. No other man had ever made her feel the way he did, as if she were a rare beauty, as if she were brilliant and utterly charming.

Priscilla discovered that all the things Pietro had told her about the prince were true for himself, as well. He was a gentle, kind and caring man.

"I wondered if I'd find you out here, miss," Mrs. Daily, the cook said, sounding winded. She wore a black dress that rounded nicely over her ample hips and a white apron. "I swear I've spent the last twenty minutes searching for you."

Disheartened, Priscilla closed the novel. She'd been found. "Is my mother looking for me?"

"No. A gentleman came to call. He gave me this card."

Priscilla examined the name and sat upright so fast she nearly toppled out of the chair. Pietro. Her heart pounded with excitement. "Has he left?"

"No. Apparently he has a letter and has been instructed to give it to you personally. He explained that he needs a reply. He's waiting in your father's den."

"Does…anyone else know he's here?"

Mrs. Daily wiped the perspiration from her brow. "Not to my knowledge."

"Thank you, Mrs. Daily," she said and impulsively kissed the older woman's flushed cheek. "You're an angel." With that, Priscilla raced across the wide expanse of groomed lawn, taking a shortcut through the garden. Breathless, she came upon the den from the outside entrance.

She stood on the other side of the double wide French doors and watched Pietro, who was standing in front of the fireplace. He seemed to be examining the carved wooden ducks her father displayed on the mantel.

Pietro turned at the sound of the door opening.

"Hello," she said, terribly conscious of her shorts and T-shirt. Her mother would most definitely disapprove, but Priscilla hadn't wanted to waste time changing clothes.

"Priscilla." She surprised him and he appeared to brace himself. At once he became stiff and businesslike. Opening his suit jacket, he withdrew an envelope.

"How are you this fine day?" she asked cheerfully.

"Very good, thank you," he returned crisply. "And yourself?"

"Great." Especially now, although it was hard to believe that the dignified man who stood before her was the same one who'd held and kissed her the night before.

"You might wish to read what's inside the envelope," he offered after a moment.

"Of course," she said, laughing inwardly at herself. It had been enough just to see him. Nothing Prince Stefano had written could rival that.

Priscilla felt his scrutiny as she read over the few scribbled lines. Either the prince had poor penmanship or he'd been in a terrible hurry. "I can't seem to make out a few lines," she said, using that as an excuse to move closer to him. "Can you?"

Pietro reluctantly read over the note. He frowned as if he were having difficulty reading the message, as well. "He apologizes for any embarrassment the article in this morning's paper has caused you."

"Did you see it?" she asked Pietro.

"No."

"Trust me, you didn't miss much. Frankly the prince is far more photogenic than I am. The article is nothing but speculation about our supposed romance, and nothing anyone with a whit of sense would take seriously. I know I'm not." She motioned toward the deep burgundy chairs that were positioned next to the fireplace. They both sat.

"Unfortunately," she confided, "that's not the case with my mother. You'd think I'd been awarded the Nobel Peace Prize from the way she's acting."

"So your parents are pleased with the attention the prince is paying you."

She wrinkled her nose and nodded. "I suppose I should let them enjoy it while they can. You see, I haven't given them that much to brag to their friends about. I'm not the least bit gifted."

His eyes snapped with disagreement. "That is most certainly not true."

If Priscilla hadn't already been in love with Pietro, she would have fallen head over heels right then. "I mean I'm not talented musically, or athletically or in some other way that parents like to brag to their friends about. With one exception," she amended, "I always achieved top grades. For years mother wanted to test my intelligence quota so she could boast to her friends that I had a genius IQ."

"Do you?" He made it sound like a distinct possibility.

"I don't know. I refused to be tested. I mean, what does it really matter if have a high IQ or don't? Knowing my test score doesn't change who or what I am, does it?"

"Not in the least."

"I didn't think so, either. Bless her heart, my mother never understood that. And so, if she can stand in the limelight with her friends because of the attention Prince Stefano's giving me, well, I figure she's waited a long time."

Pietro's gaze found hers and she smiled at him. "What was the last part of his message? I couldn't make it out."

"He's invited you and your parents to brunch tomorrow morning at eleven."

"Oh, dear," Priscilla said with a ragged sigh. "I'd hoped the banquet might be the last of it."

Pietro frowned. "The last of it?"

"The prince's attention," Priscilla explained. "Frankly, I haven't figured out what he sees in me."

Pietro's eyes snapped the way they had earlier when she claimed she was without talent. "Can you accept Prince Stefano's invitation?" he asked brusquely.

"I'm sure we can." The truth was she'd much prefer for the prince to leave Seattle, so she could quietly return to her life. But that would mean that Pietro would be leaving, as well, so she was torn.

"Before you accept, don't you think you should speak with your parents first?"

"No," she said with frank honesty. "Because if they have a conflict, I'm sure they'll make other arrangements. It isn't every day a father has a chance to foist his daughter off on royalty." It was a joke, but Pietro didn't laugh.

"If Prince Stefano chooses you as his bride, he will be the fortunate one. How is it your parents don't recognize the rare jewel you are?" He frowned, sincerely puzzled. His words were so genuine that Priscilla developed a lump in her throat. Several moments passed before it dissolved enough for her to speak.

"Oh, Pietro, you make me feel like a princess."

He opened his mouth as if he were about to speak, when the door to the den opened and her mother abruptly appeared.

"Priscilla, I've been looking for you for a solid hour. You've been hiding from me again," she said disapprovingly until she noticed Pietro.

He stood. "Good day, Mrs. Rutherford."

"Hello, Pietro," she greeted warmly, clasping her hands together. "I wasn't told you were here."

"Prince Stefano sent me to deliver a letter to Priscilla."

"A letter?" Elizabeth Rutherford's eyes brightened. "I was just looking to tell Priscilla a gorgeous bouquet of flowers arrived from the prince. Why, it's one of the largest arrangements I believe I've ever seen." She handed Priscilla the card and then gracefully slipped the prince's letter from Pietro's fingers.

Instead of reading the card, Priscilla watched her mother's eyes quickly scan the letter. Elizabeth seemed to have no problem deciphering Stefano's handwriting. "He's invited us to brunch," she cooed.

"Yes, Mother."

"I hope you told him we'd be most honored to accept his invitation."

"Priscilla has already accepted on your behalf."

"Very good," her mother said, and the "look" came over her as she studied Priscilla—one that Priscilla recognized all too well. The look that claimed there was nothing in three wardrobes full of clothes that was appropriate for her to wear. The look that said Priscilla was doomed to spend the entire day shopping.

"It was good to see you again, Pietro," Elizabeth said.

It demanded everything for Priscilla not to protest. She didn't want him to leave so soon. They'd barely had a chance to talk.

"Perhaps Pietro would like some refreshment, Mother," Priscilla said hurriedly.

"Of course," Elizabeth said, recovering quickly. "You must forgive my thoughtlessness. It was just that we're so very pleased to have met you and the prince. I was overcome with excitement to receive his latest invitation."

"I appreciate the offer, but I must be leaving."

"So soon?" Silently Priscilla pleaded with him to stay, but he looked away, ignoring her entreaty.

"I must return to the hotel to make our travel preparations."

Her gaze flew to his. "When…will you be leaving for San Lorenzo?" Priscilla asked, her voice hardly above a whisper. He'd casually dropped a bomb and then left her to deal with the aftermath. Not once had he mentioned returning to San Lorenzo. She knew, of course, now that the Romance Lovers' Convention was over, the prince and Pietro would be leaving, but she'd hoped it wouldn't be for a few days.

"We'll be returning to San Lorenzo as soon as I can make all the necessary arrangements," Pietro announced.

"And that will be…?" her mother pressed.

Pietro hesitated. "Two days, possibly three."

"Oh," mother and daughter murmured together in sorry disappointment.

* * *

Hope's day had been hectic. From the moment the alarm sounded that morning until this very second, she'd been on the run. There seemed to be a million errands that had accumulated in the past few weeks. Errands she'd been putting off.

This day had been perfect. Since she had a dentist appointment in the afternoon, she decided to make a day of it. To be fair, her motives weren't pure. She needed an escape to mull over and savor the evening she'd spent with Prince Stefano.

If she followed her usual schedule, she'd face countless questions. Although Hope hadn't said anything to Lindy about the prince, she suspected her friend had heard him ask her to meet him at the ferry terminal. And then there was her mother.

Hope wanted to avoid all the questions, all the curiosity, and so she'd used this day as a convenient excuse to disappear.

Since she hadn't taken time for lunch, Hope was famished when she finally arrived home. Checking her watch, she saw that she wasn't scheduled to meet Stefano for another three hours. Briefly she wondered if he was going to opt for the Elvis costume again this evening.

The phone rang just as she opened the refrigerator door. She groped inside for a carrot and then reached for the receiver. "Hello."

"Hope, sweetheart." It was her mother. "Are you all right?"

Hope frowned at the apprehension in her mother's voice. "Of course I'm all right. Why shouldn't I be?"

"Well...I just didn't know how you'd feel after dating Prince Stefano and everything. You seemed quite taken with him."

"Mother, I thought we already went over this." Hope hadn't mentioned anything to her mother and the other self-appointed fairy godmothers about seeing Stefano again.

"I know, it's just that...well, I didn't want you to be hurt."

Hope had to bite her lip to keep from commenting on the letter Doris had written the prince, asking him his intentions. But to do so would reveal that she'd been in contact with him herself.

"I'm fine, Mom."

"You're sure?"

The line beeped, indicating that she had another call. "I have to go, Mom."

"All right, sweetie. I just wanted to be sure you weren't upset."

"I'm not." The line beeped again and she picked up the second call. "Hello."

A slight pause followed her greeting. "Hope?"

"Stefano." She said his name in a rush of happiness.

"Where have you been all day? I've been trying to reach you for hours."

"I was doing a bunch of errands I've been putting off for weeks. You wouldn't believe all the red tape involved in operating a small business. Then I had a dentist appointment. You'll be pleased to know I'm cavity-free."

"When did you arrive home?"

"Just a few minutes ago." It dawned on her then that there could only be one reason for his call. He couldn't meet her as they'd arranged, and her heart sagged with disappointment. "You can't come this evening." She said it for him, because it was easier than to have him tell her.

"Nothing could keep me from seeing you again. I swear this has been the longest day of my life." His voice was low and sensual and it was almost as if she were in his arms again. Which was exactly where Hope longed to be.

"It has for me, too," she whispered.

He seemed to hesitate. "I'm scheduled to dine with the mayor and his wife this evening."

"Yes, I know. You already explained why we can't meet until later. I understand, Stefano. Don't worry."

"I've decided to have my driver deliver me to your home directly following the dinner. You'll be there?"

"Of course, but…"

"I'm sorry to be so rude, but I must go. I'm at the mayor's home now and they tell me dinner is being served. You understand, don't you?"

"Of course."

With that, the telephone line went abruptly dead, and Hope was left to wonder at the purpose of Stefano's call. It had all been rather odd. Yes, he'd changed their plans, but she had the sinking sensation that there was far more to this than he was letting on.

Hope chewed down on the carrot as she walked back into her bedroom and sorted through her closet, reviewing her choice in outfits. She decided upon jeans and a shirt with a Southwestern pattern.

She was examining the contents of her freezer, looking for something appetizing to zap in her microwave when she remembered she hadn't checked her messages on the answering machine.

The first was from Lindy who sounded madder than hops about something. A long beep followed and Stefano's voice came on the line, claiming she shouldn't put any credence in the article in that morning's paper.

Newspaper article? She'd brought the paper in with the mail and hadn't bothered to look at it. She went through the entire front page and didn't find a single word printed about Stefano.

Not until she reached for the society page did she see it. The photograph of the prince gazing longingly at another woman seemed to slap her across the face.

For a moment, Hope actually thought she might be ill. The impact of learning the man she loved was involved with another woman quite literally made her sick to her stomach. The blood rushed out of her face so fast that she grew dizzy.

Hope slumped into the kitchen chair and waited for the nausea to subside. Three times she attempted to read the article, and each time discovered that she couldn't get past the first five paragraphs. In those few short lines she learned that it was widely believed that the heiress, Priscilla Rutherford, had captured the Bachelor Prince's heart and that a marriage proposal couldn't be far behind.

Hope didn't know how long she sat there staring into space while she attempted to calm herself.

She was such a fool. The man was known around the world as a playboy.

How could she have allowed this to happen? That was what plagued Hope the most. Within the space of two days, she'd handed this man her heart. A man who collected women's hearts the way some do foreign stamps and coins.

He was good—she had to grant him that. He'd had her believing that he actually cared for her. Perhaps because she so wanted to believe it so desperately.

She didn't cry. This was a pain too deep for tears. A betrayal. The funny part of it was that she didn't actually blame Stefano. From what she saw of Priscilla Rutherford, the other woman was quite lovely. A woman Hope would like for a friend.

Hope had nothing to offer Stefano other than her heart. Unfortunately he was already in possession of that.

The doorbell chimed and she stared at the door for several moments.

"Hope, please." It was Stefano.

"Go away," she begged. "Just go away."

Seven

"I'm not leaving until we speak," Prince Stefano insisted from Hope's porch.

"I have no intention of opening this door," Hope said with equal conviction. He didn't know the meaning of the word *stubborn* until he'd crossed swords with her. "You played me for a fool!" she cried.

"All I'm asking is five minutes of your time," Stefano pleaded. "Hear me out and if you still don't want to see me, then I'll quietly leave."

It wasn't Stefano Hope didn't trust, it was herself. The prince made her vulnerable in ways no man had before. As much as she'd claimed otherwise, she'd inherited a romantic nature from her mother and her irrational heart had led her down a primrose path. What angered Hope the most was the way she'd obtusely followed. She was smarter than this. If she hadn't been so blinded by her attraction, she would have realized much sooner that a man like Prince Stefano couldn't possibly be serious about someone like her.

"Hope," he pleaded, "all I want is five minutes of your time."

"Answer me one thing," she insisted, finding herself wavering despite her earlier resolve. "Do you or do you not intend to marry Priscilla Rutherford?" The answer to that question would be all she needed to know.

The prince hesitated. "Let me explain."

"Answer the question." She trusted him to be honest. In light of what she'd learned, perhaps she was an even greater fool to believe Prince Stefano was an honorable man.

"Trust me, Priscilla has nothing to do with the way I feel about you."

"Stefano, if you want me to open this door, then you'll answer the question."

Once again he hesitated.

Fool that she was, Hope unlocked the door. Carrying on a conversation in this manner, with them both shouting to be heard through the thick oak door, was ridiculous.

The mesh screen door was solidly locked in place. She stood on one side and he on the other. The barrier was flimsy at best, but necessary.

Stefano's gaze held hers. She read the agony in his eyes, the pain of the truth.

"There are many things you don't understand," he whispered.

"I understand that you wine and dine Miss Rutherford and sneak away to meet me in a back alley. What you failed to realize, Stefano, is that I may be a nobody, but I have my pride, and frankly you've walked all over it."

By the time she finished, her voice was trembling. She stopped abruptly and swallowed in an effort to control her own pain, complicated by her considerable anger.

Stefano had made a mistake if he believed she would allow him to treat her in such a shabby manner.

Briefly Stefano closed his eyes. "I would rather die than hurt you."

Hope knew he spoke the truth, but why would he marry another woman if he cared so deeply for her? There could only be one explanation. He was ashamed of her. Her family wasn't good enough for the likes of Prince Stefano. Jordan wasn't a surname that brought instant recognition in the world of high society, whereas the Rutherford name was emblazoned across one of the finest shipping lines in the world.

"Are you going to marry Priscilla Rutherford?" she demanded, her voice strong and sure.

He hung his head and nodded. "Yes."

"That's everything I need to know," she whispered. With that she closed the door. For a moment, the pain of the truth was almost more than she could bear and she slumped against the wooden structure, letting it hold her upright.

Taking in a deep breath, she moved away from the door and looked out the window. Stefano had returned to his limousine. He sat in the backseat for several tortuous moments before giving his driver the order to leave.

The long, sleek automobile moved away from the curb. Prince Stefano was out of her life. He could have lied, she realized, could have glossed over the newspaper article as gossip. Instead he'd admitted the painful truth, unwilling to spare him or her with lies.

It seemed impossible that she could still love him, but she did.

Nestled on her sofa, Hope drew her knees up and rested her forehead there. It took her a while to sort through her emotions.

At first she was steamy with resentment. She was hurt. Angry. She looked for someone to blame. Her mother was the first person who came to mind. If Doris hadn't purchased that ridiculous ticket none of this would have happened.

Lindy was the second name on her list. If her friend hadn't fed her this line about romance, Hope might have seen through the smoke screen.

But ultimately there was no one to blame but herself. She was the one who'd been foolish enough to believe in fairy tales. She was the one who'd sat in a ferry terminal at nearly eleven o'clock at night, praying Stefano would show.

She was the one who'd handed him her heart on a tarnished silver platter.

Loving Stefano had seemed so right. Hope had been foolish enough to believe she had it all figured out. Him figured out. Just as if she were reading a recipe. She'd seen the look in his eyes, tasted his kisses, held him in her arms.

For a few short days she'd believed in the impossible.

It was over now. She'd made sure he understood that. All she had left were the memories, and try as she might, she couldn't make herself regret having fallen in love with the Bachelor Prince.

An hour and a half later, Hope decided against sitting inside her home on a bright, beautiful evening and brooding over her mistakes. She needed physical activity to help her out of the doldrums. With that thought in mind, she decided to water her front yard.

A bundle of nervous energy, she changed into shorts and a sleeveless top and brought the hose around to the front of the yard. Her roses needed to be clipped, and she made a mental note to put that on her to-do list for the weekend.

A roar of a motorcycle zooming down her street caused her to turn around and glare at the rider. This was a peaceful neighborhood, and the irritation of loud noises wasn't appreciated.

The rider resembled James Dean, the legendary movie actor. He wore a white T-shirt, blue jeans and black boots, and when he saw her, he roared his bike into her driveway.

"Hope."

Not until that moment did Hope realize the rider was Stefano. Her mouth sagged open in surprise.

"I can't leave matters this way between us. Unfortunately, I fear I've been followed. Come with me. Please."

"But…"

He held his hand out to her. "I will

never ask anything more of you. If you feel anything for me, you'll do as I ask without question. Hurry, please, before I'm found."

Dropping the hose, Hope leapt onto the back of the motorcycle as if she'd been born on the seat of a bike, and placed the helmet he had for her over her head. She wrapped her arms around Stefano's middle and within seconds they were off.

The prince expertly wove in and out of traffic. She saw him checking his rearview mirror several times, and when they stopped for a red light, he turned and looked over his shoulder.

"Who's after you?" Hope asked, fearing he might be in some kind of trouble.

"My bodyguard," Stefano explained.

"But don't you pay him to protect you?"

"Yes, but there are times, such as these, when I need my privacy. James doesn't appreciate that, I fear."

"How often do you come up with these disguises and the sudden need to escape?"

Stefano chuckled, but his laughter lacked any real amusement. "Only since I've met you."

"Me?"

The light changed and Stefano revved the engine, drowning out her thoughts as they continued down the busy street. Hope hadn't a clue of their destination, and she wasn't sure Stefano did, either. By the time he pulled over and parked the bike at the Ballard Locks, Hope was convinced it would take a week to clean the bugs off her teeth.

Stefano removed his helmet, helped her off the motorcycle and held her hand. They walked over to the viewing point and gazed at the long line of motorboats and sailboats awaiting their turn to travel through the locks that linked Lake Washington with Puget Sound.

"Forgive me for being so demanding," he said without looking at her. "You had every right to refuse to come with me."

That was true. "I was under the impression that if I didn't come, you'd have kidnapped me."

"I was desperate enough to have considered that, although I'd like to think myself incapable of such a crime. After this evening, I'm no longer sure."

"This evening?"

"When you closed the door on me."

It hadn't occurred to Hope that this was probably the first time anyone had behaved so brusquely with His Highness. Generally, doors were opened for him, not slammed in his face.

"I can't bear the thought of leaving matters as they were between us," he explained. His gaze studied the deep green waters as if he dared not turn and look into her eyes.

"I don't know that there's anything left to say."

"Perhaps not, but I couldn't leave without telling you the truth. I owe you that much."

Frankly, Hope had had just about all of that she could take for one day. "I know you're going to marry Miss Rutherford. You told me that yourself."

"Yes, but you do not know why."

"I'm not stupid, Stefano. Priscilla Rutherford is far more socially acceptable than I am. I own a coffee shop, remember? Not a shipping line." Although she tried to keep the bitterness out of her voice, she feared she had little success.

Stefano turned and looked at her for the first time. He framed her face in his hands and gazed deeply into her eyes. His own narrowed with an emotion she was sure she misread…love. A love so strong, it left her shaken.

"No, my love, what you're thinking couldn't be further from the truth. I must marry Priscilla Rutherford because she's an heiress."

Hope blinked. "I don't understand. You're one of the wealthiest men in the world...or so I've read. It doesn't make any sense that you'd be forced to marry for money."

He hung his head as if deeply ashamed. "It's true. My country is on the brink of bankruptcy. For the last year I've drained my family fortune in an effort to keep the economy stable. Other than a meager trust to cover my personal expenses, I'm nearly penniless."

"Oh, Stefano."

"Falling in love now is God's joke on me. You see I never really believed in love until I met you. Isn't it ironic that I should give my heart to one woman and be forced to marry another?"

Hope blinked back the ready tears that crowded the corners of her eyes.

"I promised myself a week with you. It was selfish and thoughtless of me not to have told you the truth in the beginning. I love you, Hope. I'll always love you, but within the next couple of days I'm going to walk away from you and never look back."

A tear blazed a trail down her face and she furiously wiped it aside, hating the weakness of emotion. "This is supposed to make me feel better?"

He blinked with surprise at her anger. "I...I've hurt you again."

"You couldn't leave matters the way they were? Oh, no, you had to be sure I knew you loved me. Well, that's just fine and dandy." More tears escaped, and she ran her forearm under her nose, and sniffled loudly. "This is just great."

Stefano looked utterly perplexed. "You'd rather not know how much I love you?"

"Of course I want to know that." The man simply didn't understand. "I love you, too. That much should be obvious. It's just that… Never mind," she cried. "Go and marry your heiress!" She walked several feet away from him and wiped the moisture from her cheeks while she attempted to compose herself.

She didn't hear him until he was directly behind her. He placed his hands on her shoulders and brought his lips close to her ear. "I cannot bear to see you cry."

"Don't worry about it," she said, and shrugged one shoulder. "I'm a big girl, I'll get over you. I mean…I fell in love with you fast enough, it shouldn't be that difficult to forget you." That wasn't true, but she was looking to salvage her pride by making light of her feelings.

His grip on her tightened. "Pietro wants to schedule our return flight to San Lorenzo for tomorrow afternoon," he whispered.

She stiffened. "So soon?"

"I'll agree to his schedule if you tell me you don't want to see me again. But if…if there's a chance you'd consider meeting me for the next two or three nights, then I'll rearrange my schedule to be sure I stay in Seattle a bit longer."

"You're asking the impossible," she cried. She couldn't bear to have him hold her, knowing there would soon be another woman in his arms. Couldn't allow him to kiss her, knowing he'd soon be kissing another.

"I know," he said in a tortured whisper. "We have so little time together. Forgive me, my love, for being self-indulgent. I should have realized I've asked the impossible."

"Stefano," she whispered, and her hands covered his.

He turned her into his arms and brought his mouth down to hers in a moist, gentle kiss. The pressure of his touch changed the moment Hope responded. He kissed her again and again with a growing desperation, an urgency that left her clinging and struggling for breath when he finished.

"I'm sorry," he whispered, "I didn't mean to frighten you."

He hadn't, but she didn't have the breath to assure him otherwise.

He kissed her once more, and his lips brushed her nose, her cheek, her ear. She heard a sigh rumble through his chest. He paused, seemed to draw upon his reserve of strength, and with some effort eased himself away from her.

"I'll take you home now," he said.

She nodded.

They rode back in silence, with none of the urgency with which they'd sped away. Sometime later, he came to a stop in her driveway. Climbing off the bike first, he helped her dismount and then escorted her to the front door.

Neither spoke. Their eyes met and he smiled weakly. "Thank you, Hope." He pressed his hand against her face and rubbed his thumb over the arch of her cheek. His eyes were filled with pain. "I don't know if I have the courage to walk away from you," he told her in a broken whisper.

"Then don't," she whimpered and flung herself into his arms. "Not yet. We'll worry about tomorrow later. For now we have each other."

Stefano dared not look at his watch again for fear the Rutherfords would think he was pressed for time. He wasn't. It was another three hours before he could see Hope again. If anything, he wanted the time to pass more quickly.

"I'm so pleased you could join me," he said, as the small group reviewed the menu selections. Personally, Stefano wasn't hungry. Hope had promised him a tour of the rain forest and a picnic. It would be a shame if brunch with the Rutherfords ruined that.

"The pleasure is all ours," Elizabeth Rutherford assured him. "Isn't that right, Priscilla?"

The woman seemed to prod her daughter at every turn. It had been a mistake to invite her parents, he realized. Stefano would have enjoyed the meal with Priscilla, but with her family present—especially her mother—the brunch was sure to be an ordeal.

"We are honored by your invitation," Priscilla said in a monotone, as if she'd been forced to rehearse the line countless times.

Stefano's gaze drifted toward Pietro who wore a deep frown. The prince didn't fully understand what was going on with his secretary. For years Pietro had accompanied him to endless state dinners, and other social functions. He often used his secretary as a buffer against the curious and meddling dowagers, keen on marrying him off to their daughters and granddaughters.

Stefano had sensed his secretary's reluctance the minute he asked Pietro to join him with the Rutherfords. He'd offered a weak excuse, which Stefano rejected, and afterward Pietro was tight-lipped and sullen.

Even now Pietro sat stiffly at the table as if he'd rather be anyplace else but with the prince and the Rutherfords. Frankly, Pietro's attitude was beginning to irritate him.

Stefano had once considered Pietro his friend. Now he was no longer sure. Although nothing more had been said between them regarding Pietro's resignation, it was understood that once they returned to San Lorenzo, Pietro would hire his replacement, train him and leave Stefano's employment.

Apparently the prince had committed some terrible crime, other than his treatment of Priscilla, which, frankly, Stefano didn't think was so bad.

He liked Priscilla, and knew the feeling would grow once he got her away from her mother's clutches. Already he had a tender spot in his heart for the heiress. It didn't compare to the fiery intensity of feeling he shared with Hope, but over time he believed Priscilla and he would be happy. As happy as any man could be who was in his situation.

"My husband and I were discussing your invitation to visit San Lorenzo," Elizabeth said, breaking into his thoughts.

Stefano focused his attention on Priscilla's mother. "Naturally I'd want you to stay at the palace."

Elizabeth exchanged appreciative looks with her husband as if she'd somehow manipulated the invitation from him.

"We certainly wouldn't want to intrude on your royal business," the elder Rutherford inserted.

"Darling, the prince wouldn't have

invited us if we were going to be a nuisance, isn't that right, Prince Stefano?"

"Most certainly."

"From what I understand, San Lorenzo has some of the best hotels in all of Europe," Priscilla's father said, as if he'd be just as happy in a hotel as a guest in the palace.

"That's true." Stefano didn't mention that a good portion of those world-class hotels sat vacant and were struggling to stay afloat in the current economic slump.

"If you wish," Stefano said, glancing at his secretary, "I could have Pietro arrange rooms for you at the Empress at my expense. It is our finest hotel, and I'm sure you'd be most comfortable."

"Nonsense," Elizabeth said quickly. "We'd prefer the palace. It isn't everyone who can say they've slept there, now can they?" She laughed lightly at her own joke, but Stefano noticed no one joined in her amusement.

After an uncomfortable moment of silence, Elizabeth once more picked up the conversation, directing her comment to her daughter. "You should tell the prince about your charity work, Priscilla."

"Mother, please. If Prince Stefano wants to hear about my work at the Children's Hospital, he can ask me himself."

It pleased Stefano that the Rutherfords' daughter revealed a little pluck. He was beginning to despair.

Priscilla glared at her mother and it did Stefano's heart good to see her mother squirm just a bit. He might have lessened the older woman's discomfort by inquiring about Priscilla's charity efforts, but he decided against it.

"How long will you be in Seattle?" the elder Rutherford inquired of Pietro.

"I've arranged to depart early tomorrow morning," his secretary answered.

"Change that," Stefano said.

"Change the arrangements?" Pietro asked and glared at him.

"I've decided to remain in this beautiful city for three more days. There's some sightseeing I want to do. With my current schedule I rarely have the opportunity to become properly acquainted with an area. Seattle strikes my fancy."

If looks could kill, Stefano would be mortally wounded. Pietro all but rose from his chair. Although he did an adequate job of restraining himself, Stefano wasn't fooled.

Whatever it was that was troubling his friend had gone on far too long. At first opportunity Stefano planned on confronting his secretary. The man hadn't been the same from the moment they landed in Seattle.

As it happened, the opportunity arose soon after the meal with the Rutherfords. Stefano and Pietro rode up in the elevator to the series of suites set aside for him on the nineteenth floor.

"I'd like a word with you," Pietro said the moment they were alone.

"If you insist."

"I do." It seemed Pietro was about to explode. His jaw was set and tight, and his hands were clenched at his sides.

The elevator doors rushed open and Stefano led the way into his private quarters. "What's wrong? Something's been troubling you from the moment we arrived, and I want to know what it is."

Pietro started to pace, a habit that relieved his tension. "I'd already made the arrangements to leave Seattle tomorrow morning."

Stefano shrugged. "Change them. You've done so often enough in the past. Why does it bother you so much now?"

His friend's mouth tightened. "If you insist upon staying this additional time, then I'd like to request your permission to return to San Lorenzo on my own."

"Absolutely not." Stefano didn't need time to consider his response. Not a day passed in which Stefano didn't require his secretary's assistance. To have Pietro return ahead of him would place an unnecessary burden on Stefano.

Pietro mumbled a profanity under his breath.

"Pietro," the prince said, thoughtfully studying his friend. "Can you tell me what plagues you?"

His secretary stiffened. "No."

"I can't order you, but as your friend, I would hope you could share with me what's wrong. If I've done something to offend you, let's clear the air."

"It's nothing you've done," Pietro assured him. He slumped into a chair and buried his face in his hands. "I apologize for my behavior."

Stefano could press his friend for details, but he preferred that Pietro would offer them willingly. He didn't.

"I have an appointment this afternoon," Stefano said.

Pietro nodded, without inquiring as to the prince's plans. Generally his secretary was as conscientious as his bodyguard of his whereabouts and schedule.

"Perhaps we can talk more later," Stefano suggested.

"Perhaps," Pietro agreed.

But Stefano doubted they would. It saddened him to think he had lost the best friend he'd ever had, especially when he hadn't a clue why.

Pietro sat in his compact office, staring out of the window. The view from the nineteenth floor was spectacular. Puget Sound shone like a polished jewel in the sunlight. Ferries and an abundance of oceangoing vessels patrolled the waterways. But the beauty of the scene escaped him.

A knock sounded against his door. "Come in," he called.

A footman opened the door and approached the desk. "The front desk sent this up. It's addressed to you."

"Thank you." Pietro waited until the man had left the room before tearing open the envelope. He knew before he read a single word that the message was from Priscilla.

I'm sorry to trouble you, but it's vitally important that I speak to you at your earliest convenience. I'll wait in the lobby for your reply.

He read the note and wiped a hand down his face.

After having spent an uncomfortable hour and a half in her presence, Pietro wasn't sure he could endure much more. His restraint was stretched to the breaking point. It had demanded every ounce of self-control he possessed not to make a scene with Priscilla and her mother. Elizabeth Rutherford was a fool. Somehow he didn't think the prince would appreciate it if he'd pointed it out to him.

Knowing there was no help for it, Pietro rang for the footman and asked that Priscilla be escorted to his office.

The pair returned within five minutes. It was clear that Priscilla had returned home and changed clothes. Instead of the dove-gray suit that didn't do her beauty justice, she wore a simple sleeveless summer dress and a wide-brimmed hat.

Pietro was literally stung by her beauty. It took him a moment to recover.

"Hello, Priscilla," he offered, and gestured for her to sit down.

"Pietro." She sat and clasped her hands in her lap. "Thank you for seeing me. I imagine after the spectacle this morning, you were wishing you never had to lay eyes on me again."

Actually, quite the opposite was true. The temptation to carry her away had nearly been his undoing. He couldn't tolerate the demeaning way in which her family treated her, as if her personal value rested solely in Prince Stefano's attention.

That Prince Stefano was prepared to marry Priscilla for her fortune troubled him. But seeing that he'd been the one to handpick Priscilla Rutherford from the list of potential brides, he couldn't very well object. He, too, had discredited the woman who innocently sat across from him. Now he was left to pay the piper.

"I don't mean to be a nuisance," she said, her gaze avoiding his.

"You could never be that," he assured her, hoping to keep their conversation on a professional level, and immediately failing. It was when it swayed toward the personal that he lost control. Twice now he'd held and kissed the woman who was destined to be the princess of San Lorenzo. If Stefano had so much as a hint of his feelings for Priscilla, he'd have him banished, and with reason.

"I was wondering if you could arrange for me to meet the prince alone," Priscilla asked.

"Alone?"

"Yes. Wherever we're together, there are always a number of people around… and that makes it extremely difficult for us to speak privately."

"I see." His mind was working double-time, wondering what it was Priscilla Rutherford had to say to the prince that had to be said when they were alone.

"Since it appears we're going to be in the area a few days longer than I'd anticipated, I'll see what I can do," Pietro said. He opened a small ledger where he wrote in the prince's appointments.

He paused when he saw that there was nothing written down for the prince that afternoon. Yet he distinctly remembered Stefano mentioning an appointment.

"If you'll excuse me for a moment."

"Of course."

Pietro stepped out of the office and called for a footman. "Is James with the prince?"

"No, sir. We assumed Prince Stefano was with you."

"He isn't." Pietro didn't know what kind of childish games the prince was playing, but this was getting out of hand. "Send James up to my office right away."

"Yes, sir." The footman disappeared and he stepped back inside his office and smiled at Priscilla.

"I'll contact you later with a time," he said.

"Thank you."

She didn't leave as he expected she

would. "There's something else," she said, and her shoulders rose as if it had required a good deal of courage for her to broach the subject.

"Yes?" Pietro said, looking at his watch. He didn't want to be rude, but he had a minor crisis on his hands.

"It's about—"

She was interrupted by a loud knock against the door.

"If you'll excuse me."

Defeated, she lowered her head and nodded.

"I apologize, Priscilla, but this is necessary."

"I know," she said, smiling bravely up at him.

Pietro met the bodyguard on the other side of the door and glared accusingly at the muscle-bound young man. "Where's the prince?"

"I'm…not sure."

"As I recall, this is the second time

the prince has left without your protection."

"Sir, I don't mean to complain, but how was I supposed to know the man who'd dressed up like Elvis was Prince Stefano? And then last night…"

"You mean he left unescorted last night, as well?"

"Yes. I thought you knew."

Pietro ran his hand through his hair. "No. Where did he go this time?"

"I don't know. I lost him someplace in Ballard. His motorcycle squeezed between a bus and a car, and I couldn't catch him after that."

"He was on a motorcycle?"

"Yes. From what I understand, he paid one of the hotel staff for the use of it."

Pietro splayed his fingers at his sides in an exercise in frustration. "And you don't have a clue where he is right now?"

"Not exactly."

"How about a wild guess?" Pietro was desperate. He was willing to speculate.

James shrugged his massive shoulders. "I can't rightly say."

It came to Pietro that he should fire the man on the spot, but he'd wait until later after he'd confronted Stefano. He didn't know what had gotten into the prince.

Dressing up like Elvis, riding around on a motorcycle and now this.

"I want you to report to me the minute the prince returns."

"Yes, sir," James said stiffly.

Dragging a calming breath through his lungs, Pietro opened the door and entered his office. To his surprise Priscilla was standing.

"My apologies, Priscilla. There was something you wanted to tell me."

She nodded, smiled and then casually, as if she'd been doing so for years, she looped her arms around his neck and kissed him.

Eight

Hope studied Prince Stefano's features as they stood inside the Visitor Center at Hurricane Ridge. The unobstructed view of the Olympic Mountain range with its peaks, deep valleys and ridges stretched before them, paralleling the Strait of Juan de Fuca.

Hope had never been to Europe or witnessed the splendor of the Alps, and she wondered what the prince would think of her world, so different and yet so much like his own.

"It takes my breath away," he said in awe.

"Some of those mountains remain unexplored," she told him.

"No." He raised his eyebrows dubiously. "How can that be?"

"Look at the ridges. In order to reach one mountain, you must climb a number of others. Several planes have crashed in the region, but there's no hope of ever recovering the bodies."

"How tragic. They are beautiful, these mountains of yours."

Hope smiled. "I don't exactly own them, but thank you anyway."

"You love your state?"

"Very much. Washington is quite diversified, you know. We're standing in a rain forest and in less than three hundred miles there's desert. In some areas in the eastern half of the state, the growing season is only two weeks too short for cotton."

Once more Stefano's eyebrows shifted upward. "This state of yours is amazing." His arm circled her waist. "You're amazing."

Hope smiled up at him. He hadn't worn a disguise this afternoon, at least none that required a wig. He came as himself, wearing jeans, a Western-style shirt and snakeskin cowboy boots. He looked more like a country-western star than a European prince.

"Are you hungry?" she asked.

"Famished."

She led him outside the Visitor Center. Her car was parked across the road. "There's a picnic area this way," she said, unlocking the trunk of her red Saturn.

Stefano lifted out the wicker basket and she reached for the Scottish plaid blanket. A rainbow of colorful wildflowers brightened the slopes. They trudged uphill for several moments until they found an appropriate site for their lunch. They chose a spot that offered a maximum of privacy beneath a forest of tall conifer trees.

Spreading the blanket out beneath the shelter of a Douglas fir, Hope and Stefano sat down. The area was sunny and warm and Hope welcomed the shade.

"What have you packed?" Stefano asked, kneeling down next to her on the blanket. He opened the basket and smiled when he viewed the contents.

"What's this?"

"Blueberry pie, fresh from the oven," she explained proudly. Now wasn't the time to let him know Lindy was the one responsible for this delectable delight.

"Ah, yes, American fruit pie," Stefano said. "I tasted it once in New York."

"You mean to say you don't have pies in San Lorenzo?"

"Not the way you do in America. You must remember fruit pies are a product of your country."

"But what about France? They're

known all over the world for their pastries."

"Tarts, yes, but not pie. Generally our pies are filled with meat," he explained matter-of-factly.

Hope digested this latest bit of information. "There are more differences between our two countries than I realized."

"Many, many differences." A note of sadness entered his voice and Hope knew he was thinking about his duty to his country to marry a woman he didn't love. A woman who would save his tiny country from financial ruin.

"And what are these?" Stefano brought out the thick submarine sandwiches she'd built.

Smiling, she explained the history of the oblong sandwiches. They ate then, companionably. The sun wove its way through the limbs of the Douglas fir, leaving a lacework pattern that slowly traveled over them as it crossed the brillian, blue sky.

Afterward they went on a short hike and Hope pointed out a number of different ferns. Stefano listened politely while she spread out the leaf of a sword fern, then a bracken fern and then that of the evergreen. She found herself chatting as if it were important to relay as much information about indigenous plants as possible. If she could fill the silence with words, then she wouldn't need to think about the future and how empty it would seem without him.

"Hope?"

She closed her eyes, and he pulled her softly into his arms. There was no need for words, no need to speak what was on both of their minds.

"I knew this wouldn't work," she whispered against his shoulder. She clung to him for fear that once he released her, her arms would feel forever empty.

"I thought if I kept you to myself for two more days I would have the strength to leave you. Now I wonder." His arms tightened about her. "I have no choice, my love. The fate of my country rests on my bride."

"I know. I know." Hope did, but that didn't make it any easier, loving him like this. In thinking over Stefano's plight, she'd attempted to come up with a solution that would allow them to stay together. But she could see no way out for them.

"Come," Stefano said with some effort. "Let's not think about the future. We're together now and that's all that matters."

Hope struggled to hold back the tears.

They made their way back to the picnic area. An eagle soared overhead and Hope pointed out the magnificent bird with its huge wingspan. They stood watching the eagle making a sweeping turn over the horizon. Stefano was enthralled by the grandeur of the bird that had come to represent the United States.

Sitting back down on the blanket, Hope lowered her head, fighting back the emotion. To her surprise Stefano wandered away. He stood no more than a few feet from her, but it felt as though the Grand Canyon divided them. As she watched, it seemed his shoulders slouched forward as if the weight of his burden had increased a hundredfold.

Hope did the best she could to compose herself, and once she was relatively sure she could speak without tears leaking into her voice, she stood and moved to his side.

For a long time neither of them spoke.

"I need your forgiveness, Hope," he whispered.

"My forgiveness?"

"For being so selfish. To want you so badly, to hold on to you these few days, when my presence brings you pain."

"It brings me joy, too."

"I've been unfair to you. I see that now. It is better for us both if I left Seattle."

"No." Her cry of protest came automatically. "Not yet."

"It's impossible for us. Being with you makes it even more impossible. I've done you a grave injustice and Priscilla, too. While it's true I don't love her..."

"It would hurt her if she ever found out about me," Hope finished for him.

"Yes." The lone word was barely above a whisper.

"Then she must never know." Her words were stronger and braver than her heart. She wasn't intentionally sparing the heiress who would marry Stefano. She did it for the prince. Her prince.

"You understand why this must be the last time we meet?"

"Yes," she returned in a broken whisper.

"But we have today," he returned,

gripping hold of her hand. He gestured toward the sky. "The next time you see an eagle, remember me…and that I will always love you. Hold that knowledge in your heart forever." He turned to her and cupped her face between his hands. For a long moment, he gazed into her eyes, his expression deep and troubled. "In time I fear you'll grow to hate me… that you will think me a coward," he murmured.

"I won't…I couldn't."

Briefly he closed his eyes, and shook his head. "When that happens I want you to know that leaving you has been the most difficult thing I've ever done. Please remember that, Hope, above all else. You own my heart, and always will." He paused and then gently kissed her. "As the years pass, if there's ever a time you should need me, ever a time you're in trouble—"

"No," she said, cutting him off. "It has to be over here and now, Stefano.

Promise me you won't come back into my life. You must," she insisted, before he could protest, "otherwise I'll find myself waiting for you, for the opportunity for you to return. Promise me that after today I'll never see or hear from you again."

It looked as if he couldn't make himself do it.

"Above all else, I know you to be an honorable man, Stefano. If you give me your word never to see or contact me again, then I'm free to do as you ask and treasure the days we shared. Free to take our time together and place it in the tenderest part of my heart, and cherish it. I'll be free to go on with my life."

She watched as his Adam's apple worked in his throat. "I give you my word," he whispered. "You will never see or hear from me again after this afternoon."

Hope looked away for fear he would see the tears glistening in her eyes. "Thank you," she whispered.

* * *

Priscilla knew she'd shocked Pietro by tossing her arms around him and kissing him. But she'd intended to catch him off guard. That had been part of her plan.

At first, he attempted to gently push her away, but she resisted and clung to him.

Then her hat fell on the floor and his hands were in her hair and he was slanting his mouth over hers. This must be what it would be like in heaven, Priscilla mused with a deep sigh of pleasure.

Pietro kissed her again and she gloried in his lack of control. It had happened just the way she'd planned. Once she was in his arms, he wouldn't be able to deny his feelings, wouldn't be able to brush her off with lies. He wouldn't be able to pretend.

"Oh, Pietro," she whispered, "don't stop, don't ever stop."

He stopped.

Priscilla sighed with disappointment and frustration.

They were both breathing hard, and it seemed to require several moments for Pietro to compose himself. "That shouldn't have happened," he said, his words taut with tension.

"I kissed you, remember? You did nothing improper."

"I kissed you back." He made it sound as if he should be dragged before a firing squad.

"Don't be ridiculous, I encouraged you. I wanted you to kiss me. You might think I'm being fanciful, but I knew in the beginning that you were going to be someone special in my life."

His face tensed as if he didn't want to hear what she had to say. "Priscilla…"

"You called me your love once. Remember?"

His eyes narrowed as if to say he'd give anything never to have uttered those words. "You don't understand about such things," he said stiffly.

"I understand everything I need to," she returned with a righteous tilt of her chin. "All my life everyone else—my parents, my teachers, everyone—have seemed to think they know what's best for me. And I listened. Well, no more!" She braced her hands against her hips.

"Perhaps you should discuss this with them."

"I'm going to discuss it with you."

"Priscilla…"

"Hear me out, please," she said, and as an inducement, she stood on the tips of her toes and gently brushed her lips over his. "I know now that you were lying when you said you weren't attracted to me. I'm not sure why you'd hide the truth, but that doesn't matter any longer, because I know everything now."

"About what?" Pietro challenged.

"Your feelings for me."

A sad, intense look came over him. "I find you to be an attractive, generous young woman."

"Do you often kiss attractive, generous young women the way you do me?" she challenged. She knew he didn't.

"No," he admitted reluctantly, "but then it isn't often that one throws herself into my arms."

Although he spoke without criticism, Priscilla could feel her cheeks filling with color. "What about the time before that?" she asked. "The night of the banquet. As I recall you were the one who kissed me."

"Yes, that's true but..."

Again she sensed his reluctance, his hesitation. "But what?" she prodded.

"I'm afraid I've given you the wrong impression," he murmured. "That was the night you were feeling ill and I was attempting to comfort you."

Priscilla wasn't about to accept that excuse, either. She laughed softly and shook her head. "You're going to have to come up with a better excuse than that. I may not be as worldly and so-phisticated as some women, but I know the kisses we shared were far more po-tent than a couple of aspirin."

As if he needed to put some distance between them, Pietro returned to his desk. Priscilla claimed the chair on the other side. He reached for a pen and rolled it between his palms.

"Hurting your feelings would greatly distress me, but I don't feel I have much—"

"Then don't." Priscilla felt on a natu-ral high from his kisses. Little he could say or do would discourage her now that she'd discovered the truth.

"Priscilla, you're making this diffi-cult."

"That's the reason I'm here." She beamed him a wide smile. He hesitated and looked almost grateful when the phone rang.

"If you'll excuse me a moment."

"Of course. Do you want me to leave?" she asked, thinking he might prefer privacy.

"That won't be necessary," he said, reaching for the telephone.

From her position on the other side of the table, Priscilla knew the call must be important from the way Pietro straightened his shoulders. He reached for the appointment book and flipped through the pages.

From the gist of the conversation, Priscilla could tell that he was scheduling a meeting for Prince Stefano. She couldn't be sure who was on the other end of the line, but it seemed to be some United States government official.

Pietro's look was thoughtful when he replaced the receiver. His gaze lingered there for a moment before lifting and meeting hers.

"Now, where were we?"

"We were discussing us," she said brightly.

His frowned deepened. "I didn't know there was an *us*."

"All right, I'll rephrase that. We were discussing our feelings for each other."

"I thought I'd already explained that I find you to be an attractive, likable young woman, but that I don't have any strong feelings for you one way or the other."

"I don't believe that."

He gestured weakly with his hands. "I realize that I might have given you *some* cause to think I was romantically interested in you. If that's the case, I apologize. You're a beautiful woman and I wanted to kiss you. A kiss is a little thing, don't you think?"

Priscilla blinked, her confidence shaken. "Yes, but there was a whole lot of emotion in those kisses…for me, at any rate."

"I'm honored beyond words that you find me attractive."

Find him attractive! The man didn't seem to have a clue that she was crazy in love with him. Perhaps he did, she decided, and he wanted to extract himself from the relationship as gracefully as he could.

"But," she said it for him, rather than wait.

"But you're young and impressionable, and I fear you've placed far more credence on the few times we kissed than is warranted. I don't mean to hurt you, but it would be cruel to continue in this vein."

From force of habit, she gnawed on her lower lip. "I apologize for causing you this embarrassment," she said, her pride giving her the strength she needed.

"It's not that," he said gently. "I'm honored that anyone as lovely as you would have these feelings for me."

"Yeah, right," she murmured and stood, eager now to make her escape. She turned and paused at the door. "I have an appointment with the prince tomorrow."

"That's correct."

"I'd appreciate it if I could be alone with him." In other words, she didn't want to see Pietro again.

"I'll see to it."

Her hand tightened around the doorknob and gathering her resolve, she pivoted around to face him. Their gazes met and held as if in a great unspoken battle of wills.

"Before I leave, I want you to know something." Her voice trembled a bit and she paused until she could be certain it would stay even and unemotional. "You're lying and I know it. I'm not exactly sure why you're sending me away…. Actually it doesn't matter. I'll walk out this door and we'll probably never see each other again. You've made it clear that's the way you want it, and I have no choice but to accept your wishes.

"You almost convinced me you don't love me," she continued and her voice wavered slightly, "but you didn't convince my heart."

She felt the tears burning for release and knew she had to leave soon. "Goodbye, Pietro," she whispered, and with nothing more to say, calmly left. The door softly clicked closed behind her.

Stefano returned to the hotel emotionally depleted. He met Pietro in the hallway outside his private quarters and their eyes clashed.

Instead of retreating to his own quarters, Stefano moved into the larger room where he'd shared tea with Priscilla Rutherford. Pietro followed.

For a long time neither spoke.

Stefano wasn't prepared for the litany of irate questions regarding his whereabouts. Not this time. He felt as if he'd been wrenched apart and was in no mood for an interrogation. Gratefully Pietro appeared to understand this.

"I see you're back." Pietro spoke first. "Will you be leaving again anytime soon?"

"No." Pain tightened the area around his heart. "I'd like for you to arrange our departure as soon as possible. Tomorrow, if we can be accommodated." If anything, this should please Pietro, who'd been eager to return to San Lorenzo for the past several days.

"You have two appointments in the morning," his secretary informed him. "The first is with Priscilla Rutherford."

"Priscilla?"

"Yes, she stopped by this afternoon to schedule the meeting."

"But I saw her earlier in the day. She didn't mention anything then."

"I was curious myself, but she gave no indication of what she wanted to discuss, although she made it clear she preferred that the two of you speak in private."

This piqued Stefano's interest. "In private?"

Pietro nodded. "The second appointment is with a representative from the American State Department. The call came in this afternoon and he requested an audience. He said it was essential that he speak to you at your earliest convenience."

"Regarding?"

"Again there was no indication."

"I see." Stefano was curious, but with other matters on his mind—mainly Hope—he didn't give the appointment much deliberation. Soon he'd be back in San Lorenzo. There he would find his peace. There he would have less difficulty accepting his duty. There he'd be surrounded by all that would remind him of his responsibilities to his country and his people.

"Would you like your dinner sent up?" Pietro asked, breaking into his thoughts.

"Dinner," Stefano repeated, then shook his head. "No, thanks, I don't seem to have much of an appetite." He walked toward the window, wanting the conversation to be over so he could escape.

"Will that be all for this evening, then?" Pietro inquired.

"Yes," Stefano said evenly.

Stefano could hear his secretary hesitate. "Are you ill?"

Yes, his heart cried. "I'm fine." More than anything, he wanted to be left alone.

"Good evening, then."

"Good evening, my friend," Stefano whispered, and rubbed a weary hand down his face. His secretary left the room and, after a few moments, Stefano sank into a chair and waited for the darkness of night to claim the room and his heart.

* * *

In the morning, the suite bustled with activity as the entourage that had arrived with him prepared for the flight to San Lorenzo that evening. Never had Stefano been more eager to be on his way. As soon as he departed Seattle, his heart was free to mend. While he remained in the city, his every thought centered upon Hope.

Pietro came to him around ten and it looked as if his friend hadn't slept all night. He wondered what could be troubling his companion. In light of their recent differences, he didn't feel he could pry.

Pietro's eyes were bloodshot. If he didn't know better, he'd think his secretary had been drinking. It happened rarely and generally when Pietro had something to celebrate. If he were happy it certainly didn't show.

"The front desk phoned," Pietro annnounced. "Apparently Doris Jordan and a few of her friends have asked to see you. Actually, it's more of a demand."

Stefano hesitated, unsure if he was up to a confrontation with that group. Generally he was amused by their antics, but it would take more than four romantics to entertain him this day.

"Should I have them sent away?"

Stefano hadn't the heart for that. "No." He would prefer to avoid a confrontation, but he found he couldn't refuse the fearsome foursome. "Send them up," he instructed reluctantly.

"I could meet with them, if you wish." Pietro checked his watch. "Priscilla Rutherford will be arriving momentarily."

The generosity of Pietro's offer to deal with Hope's mother surprised Stefano. "I'll keep the time in mind," he assured his secretary.

Within a matter of minutes four women marched into his suite as if they were looking to draw blood. Hope's mother, who'd swooned when she'd learned she held the winning ticket, looked anything but fragile. Her eyes sparkled with outrage.

"We want to know what you've done to Hope."

"Please sit down, ladies," Stefano instructed.

"We'll stand, thank you very much," Doris announced righteously.

The footman arrived just then, carrying a silver tea service. Another followed with a display of delicate pastries. Both were set on the table. The two footmen stood back and folded their hands behind their backs.

"Perhaps we have time for tea," the one Stefano remembered as Hazel said, tugging at Doris's shirtsleeve.

"Aren't those petits fours?" she asked as her voice dipped. "We might have been a bit hasty, don't you think?"

"Since the prince has clearly gone to

all this trouble, I think we should stay for tea," one of the others whispered.

Stefano hadn't the heart to tell them the tea had been arranged for Priscilla Rutherford.

"First answer me one thing, young man," Doris said heatedly.

In all his life, Stefano couldn't once remember being called "young man." "Of course," he said, as formally as he could, without smiling.

"I want to know why my daughter spent the entire night in tears. She wouldn't say a word, but I know it has to do with you. What have you done to her? That poor girl's suffering with a broken heart, and nothing you say can convince me otherwise. She won't even speak to me—her own mother."

"That's not the only thing," Hazel said, wagging her finger as if she were keeping time with the music. "We aren't old fools, you know. Something's been going on between the two of you ever since the night of your date."

"I want to know about the scarf she claims she got from Elvis!" Doris demanded.

"Elvis?"

The four women broke into excited chatter all at once.

"Hope Jordan?" It was Pietro's voice that cut through the prattle. His eyes linked with Stefano's and he watched as his secretary seemed to put everything together in his mind.

"Ladies, ladies," Pietro said, "I'm sorry to cut your visit so short, but the prince has an appointment in five minutes."

"But the tea..." Hazel cast an appreciative eye toward the plateful of delectable pastries.

"I don't think those were for us," Doris said, under her breath.

There was a chorus of disappointed sighs.

"Whatever questions you have for the prince can be directed to me," Pietro said. "If you'll come to my office, perhaps we can sort all this out."

Stefano shouldn't have been so grateful to be rescued from painful explanations, but it was a sign of how battered and spent he felt.

A short ten minutes later, Priscilla Rutherford was escorted into the suite. Clearly there was some sort of malady that had affected everyone, because he couldn't recall ever seeing anyone look more unhappy. She, too, had apparently spent the night pacing the floor. The circles around her eyes were dark, and even expertly applied cosmetics couldn't hide the sadness he sensed in her.

"Please sit down," he said gesturing toward the davenport.

She shook her head. "No, thank you. This will only take a moment."

Stefano remained standing because

she did. "Have I done something to offend you?" he asked, wondering at her
strange mood.

She shook her head. He noticed the
nervous way she rubbed her palms together. "I've spent a good portion of
the time since we had brunch yesterday speaking to my parents. I'm afraid
they're rather upset with me at the moment, but they'll recover." She seemed
to reach some kind of conclusion. "For
that matter," she added sadly, "so will
I."

"I'm afraid I don't understand."

"I don't expect you will." All at once
it seemed she needed to sit down because she slowly lowered herself into
a chair.

"Priscilla, are you feeling all right?"

She smiled weakly. "If you want the
truth, I've never felt worse."

"Is there anything I can do?"

She looked down and shook her head.

"I wish there was, but unfortunately there isn't."

He waited for several moments for her to speak, then prompted her. "You asked to see me?"

She nodded and slowly raised her eyes to his. "I think you're probably the most attractive man I've ever met."

"Thank you." He didn't like the sound of this. Generally, such compliments were followed by words he found to his disliking.

"No man has ever paid me the attention you have. On a bright note, you've made my mother a happy woman. My father thinks you're the best thing since sourdough bread and frankly, I don't know if either one of my parents intends on speaking to me ever again."

"What could you have done that's so terrible?" Stefano pressed gently. Priscilla was as nervous as a filly, and he feared she'd burst into tears at any moment.

She folded her hands together as if she were about to pray. "I could see the handwriting on the wall," she said, studying her fingers as though the script were written out for her there. "Mom and Dad were hearing wedding bells and I'm afraid the sound of them drowned out all reason."

"How's that?"

"You see, I like you and everything and...well, if we got to know each other a little better, we'd probably become good friends, but I don't love you."

"Love is something that's nurtured," Stefano explained thoughtfully. "After the wedding, I feel we'd develop a deep friendship, in time."

Priscilla's eyes widened perceptively. "It's true, then?" she whispered as though he'd somehow shocked her.

"What's true?"

"That you were serious about...marrying me."

He nodded. "My thoughts had been running along those lines."

"My heavens." She leapt to her feet and then just as quickly sat down again. "You see, I told my parents you had no such intentions."

"All in good time, Priscilla. I didn't intend to rush you."

"But you see, I don't want to marry you."

Funny as it seemed, her reluctance to take him as a husband had never occurred to him. There could only be one reason. "There's someone else?"

Her head bent lower, before she slowly raised her eyes to meet his. He saw in her a pain he hadn't earlier, a pain that was a reflection of his own. "There was," she admitted in a choked whisper. "But he doesn't share my feelings."

"The man is a fool."

She was saved from explaining further by Pietro who abruptly stepped into the room. His gaze honed toward Priscilla as if drawn by a powerful magnet. For a breathless moment they stared at each other, and then as though by remote control, they both looked away.

"Excuse me," Pietro murmured apologetically.

"You wanted to see me?" Stefano asked.

"It can wait." He left as hastily as he'd arrived.

Stefano watched his friend and then looked to Priscilla. She'd composed herself, but in that instant he knew the man the heiress loved, the one she wanted over him, was none other than his own secretary.

Nine

Priscilla was in love with Pietro. Stefano couldn't believe that he could have been so obtuse. The evidence was all there for him to see. Poor Pietro. No wonder his secretary had been surly and short-tempered of late. Pietro had been caught between loyalty and friendship, trapped in a no-win proposition. If Stefano hadn't been so blinded by his love for Hope, he might have been able to help them both.

Priscilla studied him, and Stefano realized he was staring at the door, after his secretary. "I appreciate your honesty," he said thoughtfully, his mind working hard and fast. "Would you excuse me a moment?"

"Of course."

"Make yourself comfortable. I'll be back momentarily."

Stefano made a hasty exit and went in search of Pietro. He found his companion in his office. "You wanted to see me?" Stefano asked.

"Has Miss Rutherford left?" It seemed Pietro's gaze bore straight through him, as if he were holding himself in tight resolve until he could be certain Priscilla had gone.

"She's waiting for me," Stefano announced and plopped himself down on the chair. "We have a problem," he announced as though the weight of this latest development were more than he could bear.

"A problem with Priscilla?"

"Yes," Stefano confirmed. "She's afraid her family is going to manipulate her into marrying me. This is the reason for her visit. She's come to explain that, although she thinks highly of me, she'd rather not be my wife. Can you believe that! The woman has no idea she's ruined our plans."

Pietro's frown deepened.

"To complicate matters, she claims she's in love with someone else—or so she says. I pried, but she wouldn't talk about him. But from what little she did tell me, she cares deeply for this other man. The cad!"

Pietro ignored the last remark. "I'm sure that in time Miss Rutherford's feelings will change. She'll grow to love you."

"We don't have the time to wait around to be sure that happens." Keeping a straight face was becoming something of a chore, but Stefano managed. "The situation is grave—you know that as well as I do."

"True." Pietro shifted uneasily in his chair.

"It's clear to me that her parents are keen on the idea of their daughter becoming my princess."

"They wouldn't object to a union between the two of you," his secretary agreed stoically.

"My thoughts precisely." Prince Stefano beamed his friend a wide grin. "That's why I believe there's only one solution to all this." He gestured with his hands, expressing his exasperation with the whole business. "We're going to need to kidnap her, and force her into marrying me."

"What!" Pietro vaulted to his feet. "You can't be serious."

"We don't have any choice. Priscilla assured me she's in love with someone else, but when I pressed her, she admitted that this other man didn't return her feelings. That being the case, we really can't allow her to throw her life away."

"Aren't you being a bit dramatic?"

"I thought that at first, but the longer we talked, the more I realized how serious she is. Priscilla's prepared to wait for this...scoundrel to come to his senses, and if he doesn't, then, well, she never intends to marry."

"She told you that?" Pietro's frown was dark and brooding.

"Why else would I be telling you this?"

His secretary wiped his hand over his eyes in a gesture of fatigue. "You can't be serious about kidnapping Priscilla."

"Desperate times call for desperate measures," the prince returned flippantly.

Pietro's fists knotted at his sides. "I won't allow it."

Stefano arched his brows in fabricated shock. "Not allow it?" he repeated slowly.

"There are laws against such matters."

"Fiddlesticks. After a month or two, Priscilla will have forgotten about the man she thinks she loves. She'll be grateful that I had the foresight to arrange our wedding. Given the circumstances, I believe her family will fully cooperate with the idea." He paused and waited for Pietro's reaction.

"I want no part of this."

"Oh, I wasn't asking you to collaborate. I was just bouncing the idea off you."

His gaze focused away from Stefano. "This is by far the most outrageous thing you've ever suggested. Are you foolish enough to believe she'll forgive you for something so underhanded?"

"It won't matter if she forgives me or not. We both know this isn't a love match. I need her money, not her." He made his voice as frigid and calculating as possible.

Pietro's eyes narrowed to points of steel. "You're a coldhearted son of a—"

He stopped himself in time to keep from swearing.

Stefano pretended to be shocked. "Why should you care? From what you claimed, your resignation will be in effect as soon as we return to San Lorenzo. You won't be around to witness any of this."

"I care," Pietro snapped.

"Apparently not enough," Stefano returned casually. He leaned back in the chair and crossed his legs.

"I was the one who chose Priscilla. You don't seriously believe I'd sit back and allow you to follow through with this preposterous idea of yours, do you?"

"Frankly, Pietro, I don't understand your objection."

"It doesn't matter if you understand it or not. I refuse to allow you to abuse Priscilla. She's warm and loving. Heaven knows she deserves better than to be treated like an object with no feelings, no heart."

The angry words fell into the silence. This was what Stefano had been waiting to hear, what he'd been waiting for his friend to admit. "Isn't that what you were planning to do?" he asked starkly. "Abandon her to a loveless marriage?"

Pietro glared at him as if he didn't understand.

"It's you she loves, you fool, not me," Stefano said smoothly. "And, no, she didn't tell me. She didn't need to. I saw the way the two of you looked at each other just now. The woman's crazy about you, Pietro, and any fool could see you feel the same way about her."

"But—"

"I believe we've already been through this argument," Stefano cut in. "She has no intention of ever marrying me. I believe she said she'd like to consider me a friend."

Pietro said nothing for several seconds, then slowly lowered himself back into the chair. "I apologize, Stefano. When I realized Priscilla was attracted to me, I did what I could to discourage her."

"Don't apologize. It's more clear to me than ever that the two of you are far better suited than Priscilla and I would ever be. You'll make her a better husband. A woman deserves a man who deeply loves her. Don't you agree?"

It took Pietro a long time to answer. "What about you?"

Stefano laughed softly. "The only thing that's injured is my ego, and that was only dented. I'll manage, and so will San Lorenzo, at least for now."

Something would need to be done to secure his country's finances, but he didn't want to think about that. Somehow he'd find a way to manage. His country had survived seven hundred years of war and plague. A little thing like financial ruin didn't seem so daunting. He'd survive without Hope, just as his country would survive without Priscilla Rutherford's money.

Priscilla shifted her weight in the chair and glanced at her watch. Stefano had already been gone several minutes, and she wasn't keen on waiting much longer. Everything she'd come to say had already been said. She hoped she hadn't hurt the prince's feelings, and frankly she wasn't willing to argue. She wouldn't marry him, or anyone, to gain her parents' approval.

The door opened from behind her just when she'd decided the best course of action was for her to silently slip away, and hope no one noticed.

"Priscilla."

It was Pietro, and the sound of his voice, saying her name in that special way of his, was enough to cause her heart to painfully constrict.

She stood and braced herself, knowing she'd need to be strong. "Hello, Pietro. Where's the prince?"

"Please sit down."

"Is the prince coming?" She looked behind him, thinking it would be much easier to maintain her composure with Stefano in the room. Otherwise, she feared she'd do something to make an even greater fool of herself than she had already.

"No," Pietro said starkly. "The prince won't be returning."

"I...see." She didn't, but it was difficult to concentrate. Slowly she sat back down, and fiercely clenched her hands together.

He claimed the chair the prince had vacated, and leaned forward slightly. "You were correct when you said I lied," he said after a tension-filled moment.

Priscilla frowned, thinking he was about to apologize for some unconfessed sin. She looked away, not having the heart for this. "It doesn't matter, Pietro."

"That's where you're wrong. It does matter. You're right, I love you, and little in this world would make me happier than for you to be my wife."

Nothing he might have said could have shocked or outraged her more. "You love me!"

"That's what I just said." He was smiling and his eyes sparked with happiness.

"You love me and...and yet you were willing to let me walk out of your life?"

"Yes," he admitted reluctantly. "Although I swear by all that is holy, it was the most difficult thing I've ever done."

"But why? Because you believed Stefano was in love with me? That's ridiculous and we both know it."

"Priscilla," he said gently, coming off the chair. He got down on one knee before her, and captured both her hands in his. "We can argue about my foolishness for many years to come if you wish. For now, all I need is your answer to my proposal. Will you be my wife?"

It greatly perturbed Priscilla that at the most important moment of her life tears would fill her eyes and blur out Pietro's face. She wiped the moisture from her face and sniffled. "There's something you should know first."

"Yes?"

"I…I have ugly feet."

Pietro burst out laughing, which was not what she'd intended for him to do. She was serious. She didn't object, however, when his arms circled her waist and he kissed her with a hunger and longing that matched her own.

"Pietro," she whispered between kisses, "you're a fool."

"Never again, my love, never again."

Ten

Stefano found a certain solace in his homeland. One that helped ease the ache in his heart. He didn't expect the longing for Hope to fade completely, and so he savored the memories of her and the all-too-short time they'd shared. Like a young boy who buries a secret treasure, Stefano clung to the memory of Hope Jordan, the woman who'd stolen his heart.

The entire country of San Lorenzo was abloom in mid-August. Although Stefano tried not to think about Hope, he found her creeping uninvited into his dreams. She came to him a vision of warmth and beauty in his sleep, when his defenses were lowered and he hadn't the strength of will to resist.

Almost always they were at Hurricane Ridge, as they'd been the last time they were together. She'd collect a bouquet of wildflowers to bring to him, her face bright with love, her eyes filled with promises he'd never collect.

Although Stefano had vowed never to contact her again, he'd hired a detective agency to report back to him with their findings. It was vital that he learn she was getting on with her life and that she was happy.

From what he'd learned, that was true. Hope's coffee delivery business was thriving, and the last and final report he'd received said that she was dating. Stefano had suffered the agonies of the damned, wondering about the young man she was seeing.

The prince hadn't returned to Seattle

for Pietro's wedding to Priscilla Rutherford. The temptation to see Hope would
have been far too strong, and he'd given
her his word that he would forever stay
out of her life. He'd honored his promise, but at a costly price.

Priscilla and Pietro's wedding was
said to have been the social event of the
year. Dignitaries from around the world
had attended the festivities. From what
the prince understood, the happy couple
were honeymooning in Australia. Stefano wished the two every happiness.

"Your Highness." His newly hired assistant, Peter Hiat, timidly interrupted
him. "Mr. Myers is here to see you."

"Ah, yes," Stefano said. "Please show
him in."

Stefano stood at his desk while the
other man was escorted into his private office. He'd met briefly with Steven Myers shortly before he left Seattle.
Myers's purpose had to do with a pro-

posal from the United States government regarding leasing land in San Lorenzo. Because of the emotional upheaval of those last hours in Seattle, Stefano had suggested the State Department contact him again, after he'd returned home.

When Stefano didn't hear immediately back again, he had assumed the project was no longer of any interest to the United States.

"Prince Stefano," Steven Myers said as he walked into the office. "I appreciate your time."

"Please sit down." He gestured toward the chair.

Myers sat and lifted a briefcase onto his lap. "Thank you for seeing me."

"The pleasure is mine. What can I do for you?"

"I've come to make San Lorenzo an offer you can't refuse," Myers said with a broad smile.

Four hours later, Stefano felt as though he were walking on air. The United States, whom Myers reminded him, had always been San Lorenzo's friend, had come seeking a favor. They were looking to establish an air base in San Lorenzo. The government of the United States was offering his country more money than Stefano had ever dreamed possible. Naturally, the decision wasn't his to make alone, but the positive side of the proposal far outweighed the negative. All it would take was a simple parliamentary vote to gain approval.

His country was saved.

Once the relief hit him, Stefano's first thought was to contact Hope and ask her to be his bride. His princess. He loved and needed her.

Then he remembered his promise to stay out of her life forever. Already she'd found another. Already she had forgotten him.

* * *

"So," Lindy said, slumping into a chair, "you going out with Cliff again this evening?"

"I wish you wouldn't make it sound like he's the love of my life. He's my cousin," Hope explained for the tenth time that day.

"I know you're related," Lindy said, biting into one of her own low-fat muffins, "but getting out again has done you a world of good. I've been worried about you lately."

This was territory Hope didn't want to traverse. Not with her friend. Especially since her own mother had been treating her as though she had a case of the measles instead of a broken heart.

Hazel and her mother's other friends were equally certain their efforts would aid Hope's recovery. They brought her jars of freshly pickled corn relish, in addition to working on a hope chest, filling it with items she'd need when she found "that special man" who would make her forget all about Prince Stefano.

As much as she loved them all, Hope felt smothered. When Cliff, a distant cousin on her father's side, arrived in town, she leapt at the opportunity to break away from the condolences being heaped upon her, and spend some time with him.

"Has Cliff found an apartment yet?" Lindy asked, carefully peeling the paper bottom off the muffin.

"I helped him move this weekend."

"Ah." Lindy's eyes avoided hers.

"What makes you ask?" Hope inquired.

Briefly, Lindy looked up and then shrugged. "No reason."

"He enjoyed the apple pie you sent over."

"He did?" Lindy's gaze widened. "Why didn't you say something sooner?"

Hope laughed and propped her feet

on the seat of the chair opposite her. "I wanted to see how long it would take you to ask."

"Hope! That's cruel."

"He asked about you, too."

"He did?"

"Yep, but I told him to look for greener pastures."

"Hope, you didn't. Tell me you didn't!"

Hope laughed. "I didn't. In fact, I gave him your phone number and he told me he'd be calling you this evening."

"He only met me the one time...." Lindy's hands nervously set aside the muffin.

"You made quite an impression on him. Then again, it might have been the apple pie," she said, giggling. It felt good to laugh again. She hadn't had much reason to laugh of late, but she was learning.

The bell above the door to the coffee shop sounded and Hope plopped her feet onto the floor. "I'll get that," she mumbled. This was the first break Lindy had taken all morning, and Hope didn't want her friend to wait on walk-in customers. Not when the kitchen demanded so much of her time.

"Hello," Hope greeted the smiling young woman. She looked vaguely familiar, but Hope couldn't place her. "Can I get you something?"

"You don't know me," the other woman said, extending her hand. "I'm Priscilla Rutherford—or rather, that was my name. I recently married Pietro. You know him as Prince Stefano's secretary."

Hope's body froze. *Not now,* she silently begged. *Please not now. Not when I'm just getting my life back together. Not when I've convinced myself I can be happy without him.*

"How can I help you?" she asked

once more, stiffly this time, protecting her heart as best she could.

Priscilla smiled gently. "You can't. Pietro and I are here to help you."

Three weeks following their marriage, Pietro and Priscilla arrived home at the palace.

"Pietro," Stefano shouted when he first saw his friend. He rose from behind his desk and the two men exchanged hearty hugs. Stefano briefly kissed Priscilla's cheek. It amazed him how radiantly beautiful the heiress looked. Apparently, married life agreed with them both. Pietro had never looked better.

"I thought you two were on your honeymoon," he said, ringing for the footman, and ordering a tray of coffee to be sent up.

"We cut it short," Pietro explained. Husband and wife sat next to each other, holding hands. "We read about the agreement between San Lorenzo and the United States," Pietro explained. "It made the Australia newspapers. It's true isn't it, about the air base?"

"Yes." Stefano beamed Pietro a smile. "We're more than pleased. The parliament voted on the proposal in record time, and construction is scheduled to begin on the project after the first of the month."

"Congratulations."

"I'm grateful for the turn of events." Which was an understatement only Pietro could fully appreciate.

"What about the wedding?"

Stefano stared at his friend. "Wedding? Whose wedding?"

"Pietro," Priscilla said softly, casting a disapproving glance toward her husband, "you're going to ruin the surprise."

"Surprise?" Stefano was beginning to feel like a parrot, repeating everything said.

"We brought you back something from our honeymoon," Pietro explained. "Would you like to see it?"

"In a minute," Stefano said. He was more eager to talk to the two. He'd deeply missed his friend. His newly hired secretary was efficient and organized, but he lacked Pietro's skill in several areas, the least of which was the sword. It'd been weeks since Stefano had been challenged. Never had he felt more alone than in the past month without Pietro at his side.

"Tell me about the wedding," Stefano instructed.

The footman delivered a silver tray with a pot of coffee and three cups. Priscilla poured, while chatting.

"First off, Mother and I had quite a discussion. She wanted a wedding that would rival something coming out of Buckingham Palace."

"It didn't help matters," Pietro said, smiling at his wife, "that you had me knighted before the wedding. Elizabeth felt that if Priscilla was going to marry a knight, she should have a wedding fit for a queen."

"Despite everything, the wedding was lovely," Priscilla assured him.

"We missed you, however," Pietro said.

"My mother was convinced you didn't attend the wedding because I'd broken your heart by choosing Pietro over you."

"That's very nearly true," Stefano returned, and shared a secret smile with his former secretary. "Now, what is it you're so eager to show me?"

"Shall we make him close his eyes?" Priscilla asked her husband.

"I don't think that's a good idea." Pietro stood and walked over to the large double door and disappeared momentarily. When he returned, Stefano was convinced he'd lost his mind—he couldn't believe what he saw.

Hope Jordan stepped into the room and smiled serenely at him.

"Hope." He rasped her name as if he were saying a prayer, pleading to the powers on high.

"Hello, Stefano."

He couldn't believe how lovely she was. Had he forgotten so much about her, so soon? It was as though she were a vision, a figment of his imagination.

"You might want to ask her to sit down," Pietro prodded.

"Of course. Forgive me."

"Pietro, don't you think we should leave these two alone for a few minutes?" The sound of Priscilla's voice drifted to Stefano but it seemed as if it were coming from a great distance.

"I suppose.... We'll be waiting in the rose garden," Pietro said as he followed his new bride out the door. Stefano barely heard his friend.

Each one of his senses was centered on Hope. "I wasn't sure I should come," she said, and for the first time he realized she was ill at ease.

"Not come?" He sat across from her.

"I wasn't sure your feelings for me hadn't changed."

"They haven't. You hold my heart in the palm of your hand. You always will."

She lowered her head and he noted the nervous way in which she nibbled at her lower lip. "You didn't contact me. Not even after you learned about the air base. I'd never have come to San Lorenzo if it hadn't been for Pietro and Priscilla."

"I'd given you my word of honor that I'd never see you again."

"But that was when you were planning to marry Priscilla Rutherford. That was when there was no future for the two of us. I thought…when I learned about the air base, what else could I think but that…well, that I'd been a passing fancy who'd amused you while you were in Seattle."

"Hope, no. Never that." He'd hurt her so much already, knowing he'd caused her additional pain brought a surge of bitter regret.

"Then why didn't you come for me?"

It wasn't easy to admit what he'd done. "I learned you were dating, and felt it was best to let you get on with your life. I'd hurt you already."

"You learned I was dating! Who told you that?" She sounded agitated, as well she should.

"I'm not proud of this…but you need to understand my state of mind. I hired a detective agency to check up on you." He drew in a deep breath and held it for fear she'd never forgive him for invading her privacy. "I had to know that you were well…I couldn't have gone on without that peace of mind."

"Oh, Stefano…"

He couldn't resist holding her a moment longer. He gathered her in his arms and absorbed the feel of her, her softness, her gentleness. Her love. For weeks Stefano had felt as if he were adrift on a wide ocean with no land in sight. He'd suffered deeply, believing Hope had found another man. He'd been torn in different directions, seeking her happiness above his own.

They kissed and it was as it had always been between them. Soon his hands were in her hair and he was drinking in the taste of her, the feel of her.

"Promise me you'll never leave me again," Hope asked.

"On one condition." He kissed her, not giving her time to respond for a long, long time.

"Anything you ask," she said with a sigh between deep, slow kisses.

"Marry me. Stand by my side the rest of my life. Be my princess."

"I'll need to think about it," she whispered. Stefano lifted his head, surprised by her response. She smiled up at him, wove her fingers into his thick hair and laughed softly, before bringing his mouth back to hers. "I thought about it."

"And?" With a great deal of restraint, he held his lips a mere inch away from hers.

"And, the answer's yes. A thousand times yes." Stefano let out a triumphant cry, wrapped his arms around Hope's waist and whirled her around. It was a fitting gesture, since she'd sent his world spinning from the first moment he'd seen her. He had a sneaking suspicion this was one joyride that was never going to end. The Bachelor Prince had met his match. His mate for a lifetime.

* * * * *

ESSENTIAL COLLECTION

YES! Please send me the *Essential Collection by Debbie Macomber* in Larger Print. This collection begins with 3 FREE books and 2 FREE gifts in the first shipment, and more free gifts will follow! My books will arrive in 8 monthly shipments until I have the entire 51-book *Essential Collection by Debbie Macomber*. I will receive 2 or 3 FREE books in each shipment and I will pay just $4.99 U.S./$5.89 CDN. for each of the other 4 books in each shipment, plus $2.99 for shipping and handling. *If I decide to keep the entire collection, I'll have paid for only 32 books because 19 books are FREE! I understand that by accepting the 3 free books and gifts places me under no obligation to buy anything. I can always return a shipment and cancel at any time. My free books and gifts are mine to keep no matter what I decide.

261 HCN 1446   461 HCN 1446

Name	(PLEASE PRINT)	
Address		Apt. #
City	State/Prov.	Zip/Postal Code

Signature (if under 18, a parent or guardian must sign)

Mail to the **Harlequin® Reader Service:**
IN U.S.A.: P.O. Box 1867, Buffalo, NY 14240-1867
IN CANADA: P.O. Box 609, Fort Erie, Ontario L2A 5X3

EDMBPA14